TROUBLE WITH THE LAW

The Major rode down to the city jail, tied the animal outside the shoddy building, and went inside.

There was a man on duty at the desk. He looked up as The Major came in and yawned: "What's your problem, bub?"

Dorne did not like being called that, especially by a redneck police sergeant. "I'm looking for a friend of mine."

The man looked him up and down from his flat-crowned hat to the fringed buckskin jacket. "What's the name?"

The Major hesitated. "He's Irish, big . . . broken nose. . . ."

"You've gotta nerve. Get out of here before I throw you in a cell and pitch the key away."

The next second the startled sergeant was staring down the barrel of The Major's gun. "Don't try to be funny. Just get up out of that chair and show me around."

The sergeant made a mistake. He tried to grab for the gun. . . .

Other *Leisure* books by Todhunter Ballard:

INCIDENT AT SUN MOUNTAIN
GOLD IN CALIFORNIA!
THE CALIFORNIAN
FIGHT OR DIE

TODHUNTER BALLARD

TWO TONS OF GOLD

LEISURE BOOKS   NEW YORK CITY

A LEISURE BOOK ®

November 2003

Published by special arrangement with Golden West Literary
Agency.

Dorchester Publishing Co., Inc.
200 Madison Avenue
New York, NY 10016

ISBN 0-8439-5291-1

Visit us on the web at www.dorchesterpub.com.

TWO TONS
OF GOLD

Foreword
by
Sue Dwiggins Worsley

Phoebe Dwiggins and Todhunter Ballard were distant
cousins who saw each other frequently because Phoebe's
mother, Betsy, was an avid bridge player. Tod, who liked
bridge as much with worthy opponents, would often join
this afternoon bridge group at the Dwiggins' home in
Nichols Canyon, Hollywood. Following the afternoon
games, Tod would usually spend the evening there. Before I
met Phoebe, I met her brother Don Dwiggins when he, as
city editor of a college newspaper, gave me my first assignment. Shortly after that, on our first date, Don's fraternity
group used the Nichols Canyon house as a meeting place
before going to a dance, and I met the whole family. Not
long after I was invited to one of their big parties—mostly
writers, artists, and musicians. I was in love with the whole
"clan" before being in love with Don. We were married in
1935.

Phoebe was a painter, both portrait and landscape. Tod
as W. T. Ballard was already a successful pulp magazine
writer. I was totally in awe of him. He knew all, or nearly
all, of the famous writers who were being published in the
pulps, among them Dashiell Hammett and Raymond Chandler. In fact, Captain Joseph T. Shaw, who edited *The Black
Mask*, asked Tod's opinion of the first story Raymond
Chandler submitted anywhere, and Tod recommended it

for publication. Tod and Phoebe were married in 1936.

Tod had graduated from Wilmington College in 1926. His father had been one of the early casualties of the Depression. Fred Ballard had once been a highly successful engineer with a prominent company. After the crash, he could not find work and never really adjusted to the disaster of his financial losses. Tod was almost the sole support of his parents and, at least, one other relative. By 1929, Tod had been writing and successfully selling his fiction for some time, but he was not so well established that he could depend upon writing as his sole income. When I first met him, Tod had already worked for a couple of Hollywood studios, and had tried his hand at numerous other kinds of jobs to earn a buck. One memorable story about Tod's varied working background occurred in the living room of the Nichols Canyon house while the four of us were living there. Don and Phoebe's parents were, as usual, at Canada Lake, N.Y., for the summer. Tod was doing well enough at the time that he had hired a secretary named Peggy. It wasn't long before she became a member of the family and moved in—with her recently acquired golden retriever. Peggy was an excellent secretary, but was one of the most naïve individuals I ever met. She was such a fan of Tod Ballard's that she'd named her dog William Tecumseh Lennox—or Bill Lennox, for short—after the hero of many Ballard short stories and of his first novel, SAY YES TO MURDER (Putnam, 1942).

Some friends had joined us in the living room at the end of the day's work, and one of them started asking Tod about his background. In the course of answering, Tod mentioned a number of the jobs he'd held—ending up with a description of a short-order joint to illustrate the gamble of going into business for yourself. Peggy had been listening raptly, and, as he finished his point about the short-order joint, she burst out, wide-eyed and serious: "Tod, how old are you, anyway?"

He said: "Why?"

"Well, ever since I've known you, I've heard about all the jobs you've had and all the interesting things that have happened to you, and, well, you've gotta be older than I thought you were."

The laughter exploded. Neither Peggy nor Tod lived it down as the "how old are you" story made the rounds. Actually it was true he had done an astonishing number of jobs, no matter how short-lived, and he was the kind of person who learned all about anything he ever worked at, down to the smallest detail. It undoubtedly was a trait that greatly added to his success as an author.

I'm not sure how long it was before Phoebe was actually writing with Tod. She had given up painting, much to my disappointment, within the first year of her marriage to Tod. Working with him had started, naturally enough, with her typing his finished copy. He was a two-to-three finger rapid typist. When he was really going full blast—and that was a good part of the working day—he turned out a lot of copy, but, of course, it needed to be cleaned up.

Phoebe's name seldom appeared on a book of Tod's, and he finally gave up trying to get credit for her. Publishers considered his name marketable, not hers. The same practice has been followed with regard to this unpublished manuscript. Yet, although Phoebe's name doesn't appear anywhere on TWO TONS OF GOLD, never doubt that she worked on it. Already by the end of the first year of their marriage, the Ballard team's method of working had become well established. With rare exceptions, the two were up and having breakfast between 7:00 a.m. and 8:00 a.m.

and that breakfast rarely varied—bacon, eggs fried in bacon grease, toast, and coffee—a thing to horrify modern nutritionists, but they both lived into their eighties. Wherever they lived, they arranged it so that they could work in separate rooms, each with a typewriter. From time to time Tod also used a Dictaphone (there weren't small tape recorders then).

Once during a two-month period during which I was between jobs, I worked with them at their apartment. We had three rooms set up. I transcribed from the Dictaphone, pretty much *verbatim,* and Phoebe took those pages to do a re-write and prepare the finished copy. Doing finished copy for Tod involved some re-writing but also a good deal of interpretation. If you were to ask him how to spell a word, he'd spell it. But, when he was actually writing, he thought and typed so rapidly once the plot was in his head that sometimes it was a guessing game to decipher which word he had chosen. Eventually even I came to be pretty good at deciphering this Ballardese. They were such a good team. The usual routine was: a story conference to set the general background, characters, and plot. Tod then did the first draft, Phoebe took over for the second, and then, of course, there would frequently be more conferences about changes. Over a period of years, I was lucky enough to be asked to join in on some of their story conferences. It was an education and great fun.

Looking back, the Depression did bring out attitudes and actions in individuals that one might not see so readily in more bountiful times. Among the people I knew, especially the writer group, there was a real concern each for the other. They kept in touch, and, if the word went out that someone needed money or help, somehow it was provided. To illustrate the point, the Ballards became intrigued with

Azusa, a little town east of Los Angeles. A couple of writers had bought inexpensive lots there and built their own places. The Ballards decided it would be a good investment, and, since they had a little money saved, they bought a lot. Like most of the lots in that area, theirs encompassed about an acre. They decided to do the building themselves. What they hadn't already learned doing repairs at various family places, they learned as they went along. They took time off from writing for enough days to get the foundation, flooring, and a roof done. By then, it was warm weather, so they could really camp out comfortably with that much done. Then they used the mornings for writing and the long afternoons for the building project.

By this time, besides Peggy, Tod had also acquired a young male amanuensis. Earl was familiar with Tod's books, in fact had looked him up because he wanted to be a writer and was willing to do anything to learn from Tod. Tod's first words of advice to Earl, as to anyone else who might ask him how to become a writer, was: "Put the seat of your pants to the seat of your chair and stay there until you've written something." So it became a foursome to do the writing and building. One corner of the place was set up for the kitchen; in another corner was a mattress for Phoebe and Tod; in the third corner was Peggy's mattress; and in the fourth was Earl's. Peggy had her mattress carefully draped off with sheeting—she was a very modest young lady. Against one wall was the "office", consisting of chairs, typewriters, and so on.

The next most urgent building job was to get a cesspool dug so they wouldn't be so dependent on arrangements suitable only for camping out. They decided that if they took several days off—not doing the usual morning hours of writing—they could get the job done. It was hard physical work, and it was hot. But they stuck to it, and by the end of the second day it looked as if they'd be finished by the next day. They all bedded down early, exhausted. Sometime in the middle of the night, Tod was rudely awakened by Peggy—modest Peggy—standing over him with just a towel clutched to her bosom. She was tugging at his shoulder and imploring him: "Tod, get up . . . get up . . . there's someone out there. I hear him!"

Tod was only partially awake. "Who? Hear him what?"

Peggy: "Digging . . . I hear him digging."

Tod: "Digging? My God, don't stop him. Never stop a man with a shovel!"

Phoebe: "Amen! Get in here beside me and get some sleep. We'll see how much he's done in the morning."

Of course, all they found the next day were some animal tracks and spoor. They still had to finish the job themselves. That episode resulted in a family by-word—"Never stop a man with a shovel."—that was readily adaptable to many other lines of endeavor: a pickaxe, a lawn mower, or, for that matter, a typewriter.

On the day they finished the cesspool, a writer who they had met only once before arrived with his girl friend to see how things were going. The Ballard digging crew was in high spirits over the job they had done and invited the guests to stay for dinner. The guests had brought beer and some munchies, and they all sat around telling stories until about 10:00 p.m., when the guests left.

I was working at M-G-M in the Sound Department, and Don was working for John Hix on STRANGE AS IT SEEMS, and we hadn't had a chance to visit the Ballards or have a barbecue with them for about three weeks. I got a call from the girl friend of the writer. Since I hardly knew her, I was a little surprised to have her call me at work. She started out with small talk, seemed embarrassed, and finally said: "I hope you'll understand why I'm calling. I never butt into other people's business, but how long is it since you've been out to see the Ballards?"

I said it had been quite a while, and, since they still had to use a public, or neighbor's, telephone, I didn't talk to them. Why was she asking?

After some more hemming and hawing, she blurted out that I mustn't ever tell them. She didn't want to embarrass them, but she was afraid they were having a bad time, even going hungry, and were too proud and brave to call for help. She went on to tell about having gone out there yesterday, and that all they had had was beans. She had quietly looked around, and there didn't seem to be much food of any kind in the icebox or the cupboard where they kept things. I thanked her for calling and said I'd find out what was going on.

I called Don, filled him in, and we went out that night, taking steaks, potatoes, and corn to roast on the barbecue, and even some canned goods just in case the gal was right, although we couldn't see why the Ballards wouldn't yell for help. When we arrived, they'd just finished working—the barbecue was already lit and there were steaks as well as chicken parts ready to go on it. A big salad had been made, and they were having drinks. They were delighted to see us but were somewhat surprised by all the things we had brought. Just steaks and beer would have been fine, but all the canned goods! Phoebe asked if we were planning to move in?

So we told them, and they laughed. They laughed so hard they could hardly talk, and then they told us about digging the cesspool and finally finishing it just before the writer and his girl friend had arrived.

13

Phoebe said: "If we hadn't been so tired, we'd have cleaned up and taken them to dinner, but there were enough beans for all of us, so we made do."

The Ballards were meticulous researchers, especially in regard to the many novels with a Western background. For GOLD IN CALIFORNIA (Doubleday, 1965), which received the Spur Award from the Western Writers of America, and THE CALIFORNIAN (Doubleday, 1971), they spent at least six months living in Sacramento and driving through and exploring the gold country in addition to using the library there. A few years later, they actually got involved in a gold mine partnership with another couple whose names I've forgotten. They spent another six months living there and helping to work the mine. It wasn't a hardship camping out, but it wasn't ordinary housekeeping, either. They didn't really make any money out of the project, but obviously they loved the adventure and learned even more about gold mining.

There were few times in the Ballards' marriage when they weren't writing full-time. The most extended period was during World War II. Tod was recruited to work at the big Wright Patterson Army Air Force base at Dayton, Ohio. It was the summer of 1943. One of our friends was stationed there, working in a heavily classified area. When he realized they were looking for civilian help, he recommended Tod. Tod was unable to enlist due to disability from a childhood bout of infantile paralysis (better known later as *polio myelitis*). He had a slight clubfoot and had some impairment of one hand, but it didn't keep him from doing most things.

The Ballards notified all of us. They packed up and within two days were on Highway 66, heading east. In a single day they arrived to visit us in Holbrook, Arizona

14

where we were stationed. They could only stay the night. Tod's orders were to get to Ohio as soon as possible. He didn't know what he would be doing except that it was classified, so we didn't find out even after he knew. Over the next couple of years we corresponded and very occasionally managed phone calls (telephones, like new cars, were hard to come by in those days). The professional writing was severely restricted. Tod was too busy to spend much time at it, so mostly they used week-ends for story conferences. Phoebe would get a draft made, and they'd just work on it when they could.

There was a four-year hiatus between the publication of Tod's first hard cover novel, SAY YES TO MURDER, and the second, MURDER CAN'T STOP (McKay, 1946). In between, I think, they only managed some magazine stories. They left Wright Field after V.E. Day, going to New York to mend fences with editors, publishers, and confer with their agent, August Lenniger. They didn't get back to California until after we did, in August of 1945, after the war had ended. I can't prove it, but I'm sure the typewriter was clacking away and the words were tumbling out within days of their arrival home.

In 1959 I was seriously thinking about quitting my job in public relations and getting back into movie studio work. Tod and Phoebe were swamped with orders, and he made me a deal. They would pay me the same salary I was getting. I could work with them and still look for other work, going out on interviews. Besides, he was looking for new background for a novel, was thinking of publicity, and thought I could supply him with information and stories about the Hollywood variety. It was one of the most gratifying jobs I ever had. The story conferences were really great. They were both open to ideas and criticism, and it turned out to be rewarding for me to learn more about writing. I stayed with them about six months, and we were working on a Western, when the job that I wanted came my way. We had a good laugh about it. It was a Western television series, "Wichita Town" (NBC, 1950), with Joel McCrea. It only lasted one season, but the production outfit was a great one to work with—The Mirisch Company.

Tod died in December, 1980. I had visited them in Mount Dora, Florida at Thanksgiving time. He was ill, had been for some time, but we actually did some story conferencing because I'd been struggling with the beginnings of a novel. Between the two of them, it didn't take much time to point out my problem. He and, long since, Phoebe had become great story doctors.

We took Tod to the hospital on Thanksgiving morning. He never got back home. I said good bye to him in the hospital before I returned home.

Phoebe died in October, 1991 in Woodland Hills, California—a hop, skip, and a jump from me. I still miss them—a lot!

Chapter One

Death rode the Washoe Zephyr on that hot and windy day. Blood stained the blistering dust of C Street, and the heat-shimmering air of Sun Mountain, Nevada stank of spilled lives. Fifty strike-breaking Hounds, recruited from the dregs of San Francisco's Barbary Coast, overran ten striking miners where they picketed the Calico Mine and beat them to death before the eyes of their womenfolk.

The ten bodies lay in a row on the wooden sidewalk before the office of the *Territorial Enterprise*, surrounded by a silent, stunned throng of off-shift men and newly made widows when the stage from Placerville rolled down the grade and stopped.

A tall man dressed in a major's uniform remained for an incredulous moment in the stagecoach doorway. Under a cavalry slouch hat, his dark hair was abundantly streaked with pure silvery white, providing a startling contrast to the young face and penetrating black eyes. Finally he swung down and strode forward, shouldering through the wall of backs to the edge of the boardwalk. There he came to a sudden halt, looking down into the face of his father, where blood still oozed to paint a strip of red in his white hair.

He turned, eyes searching for and quickly finding his mother. He shoved through to her. For a long moment they looked at each other, her eyes black like his but expressionless. His stunned reaction to the whole scene deepened. Somehow, he knew, she would not know him again.

He acknowledged the friends surrounding his mother

17

and left her in their care, thankful for their understanding offer to get her home and care for her until he could come. They knew him—Major Mark Dorne, on leave from duty, only stopping to see his parents on his way to a new post in Montana. They knew his story—through the Civil War he had been the youngest major in the Union Army and held that rank when peace returned. He had chosen to stay in the service. For five years he had moved from fort to fort, an ordnance officer, an expert at demolition.

Now he reached the sidewalk, crossed it into the *Territorial Enterprise* newspaper office. The editor, Arthur McEwan, was an old friend. He was waiting, offered a hand, and said in a hushed voice: "Terrible. Terrible . . . and more to come."

Dorne's tone was flat, without expression. "Who? Why?"

Young Arthur McEwan looked older than his years today, drained of his fine energy and shaken to his boot soles. A man of great editorial courage, he minced no words.

"Strike. The miner's wages are being cut to a rotten three fifty a day. The fat cats of Montgomery Street think they're not raking enough cream off the hill."

"Who's behind it?"

"A new company. Union Mining and Milling. When the mines were down, the Bank of California came in and loaned the mills a lot of money, and now they're foreclosing. They've got nearly every mill in town, taking over and slashing wages."

"I said who? What men?"

The editor spat names. "Bill Ralston is cashier of the bank. Bill Sharon is local head of Union Mining and Milling. He runs Virginia City and the state like personal property. Water, timber, you name it, they control it all."

"And murder men wholesale. How do they think they can get away with it?"

McEwan looked bleakly at the major. "They own the courts, too. The legislature. The governor. They'll claim the pickets were trespassing on private property, and butter won't melt in their mouths as they say it. But nobody will raise a hand against them. Except me. I'll write the god-damned story for the world to read."

The cold knot in Dorne's stomach tightened. While he was serving his country, these greedy robber barons had been raping the land with impunity, killing with impunity, and had become gods over the fates of men by virtue of the power of usurpation, because there was no force powerful enough to stop them.

McEwan indicated a list—headed by his own name—a starting list of volunteers. Dorne silently added his own name—as one who would stand with them.

He left the newspaper office and went to the post office. There he wrote to Scofield Barracks in St. Louis from which the 7th Cavalry had been recruited.

Dear Sirs:
  I hereby resign my commission in the United States Army. I am enlisting in a war of my own.
                                        Very truly yours.
                                   Mark Dorne, Major,
                                   7th Cavalry, U.S. Army

At the small but well-built house of his parents, he found his mother sitting very still in the rocker which was her usual resting place. His father's chair stood empty. Two women, obviously having taken over the care of the be-reaved woman and her house, carefully avoided sitting in

Patrick Dorne's chair. They told Mark Dorne ten caskets were even now being built and would be ready by morning.

It was scarcely daylight when they climbed the barren mountain. His mother moved in the silence that had possessed her from the moment she knew her husband was dead. She neither accepted nor openly refused help.

They buried Pat Dorne in the flinty soil the miner had worked so long. Looking down on the plain, closed coffin, the major made a low-voiced vow. "They will not forget you. I promise that. They will remember."

It took a day or so to provide for his mother's care, arranging for one of the other newly made and destitute widows to live there and putting McEwan in charge of funds to care for them both.

Then he began a new life.

Chapter Two

After each raid against the vast mining and milling company or one of its affiliates, Dorne left a silver dollar. The coin was not of the same design as those the government minted. It was manufactured by one of the private coinage companies that had grown up in San Francisco during the gold rush and was still doing business. One side featured an image of a bloated figure with the inscription: **In Boodle We Trust.** The other side featured a hangman's noose, with the words: **Pat Dorne—Murdered at Calico Mine.** A loop of wire was threaded through the edge of the coin, allowing for easy attachment in any handy, obvious place.

With every coin delivered to his desk, William Sharon, who ruled the mountain for the Bank of California, cursed and thundered and sent gunmen out to stop the vandals. Each time those who came back from the search reported it was like hunting a ghost.

Strikes occurred all across the territory wherever the mining ring claimed property, but it was always in some unexpected place. A mysterious figure that people called The Major was seen in each of the areas before or after a raid. He was described as more a shadow than man, dressed in fringed buckskin such as Custer had made famous, black in color instead of dun. He wore a cavalry slouch hat. His hair color was reported as brownish, or grayish, depending upon the description of the various reporters. But all were sure of one thing, he carried an arsenal. It was said he wore two revolvers, holstered at his hips, a Derringer with a four-barrel revolving action in a coat pocket, a rifle in a sling over his shoulder, a Greener with two three-foot barrels that hurled .50 caliber slugs, and it could be mounted on a folding swivel, an arrangement hanging from his belt—and, as a finishing touch, knives in the tops of his boots. Sometimes he wore a strange vest decorated with short yellow tubes.

William Sharon didn't believe one man could carry such an arsenal. Sharon could conjure up the picture of the man but not accept it as a reality. However, the losses in silver were very real, and The Major, with or without the storied arsenal, had to be stopped.

While Sharon planned for his capture, The Major sat patiently waiting, his back against the bole of a great tree in the Ponderosa stand that lay west of the High Sierra range and above the winding stage road between Virginia City and Placerville. To the west, within his sight, squatted the buildings of the stage station at Strawberry. The stage company had hacked out a lifeline across the mountains to the Comstock Lode. The dusty ribbon of the road snaked past The Major just a hundred feet below.

Over that road flowed all the supplies that fed the thirty thousand miners, storekeepers, saloon men, boarding house managers, and all the equipment, heavy and light, that was needed to keep Virginia City functioning night and day. In the opposite direction the road was in sight for some distance. From that way the river of silver—gutted from the bowels of Mount Davidson, locally called Sun Mountain—was hauled to the outside world.

Every month a shipment went over the mountains to the bank in San Francisco where the heavy bars were transformed into coins deposited into the Bank of California's coffers. The treasure wagon due today would never reach its destination. Mark Dorne needed more silver, needed the bright bars for his war chest, to continue his siege against what the newspapers were calling "Ralston's Ring," a consortium of the greediest business pirates ever combined to rape the resources of the land.

At his side rested a wooden box filled with yellow sticks of a soft putty-like substance. As a demolition man the Army had sent Dorne to Sweden to consult with an associate of Alfred Nobel, the chemist who had invented nitroglycerin, a highly explosive syrup destined to revolutionize methods of excavation and even war. In its liquid form nitroglycerine was treacherous to use. Dorne and Nobel's associate had experimented and developed a stabilizer to complement it, mixing nitroglycerine with *Kieselguhr,* the fine-grained diatomaceous earth that was the siliceous residue left by millions of years of marine algae deposit. Molded into long rolls, the dough could be wrapped in a cardboard sleeve and detonated by another Nobel invention, a cap to be pressed into the end of the stick and activated by a fuse, a hollow, pliable tube loaded with gunpowder. When the powder was lit by a match, a little flame snaked along the fuse.

Nobel named his product dynamite and patented it in France in 1867 and in America in 1868, but very little of it was shipped into the country in the next two years. Mark Dorne did not need it shipped to him. He could nitrate the glycerol and mine the *Kieselguhr* himself and had been doing so since his personal war had begun. The deadly supply was stashed and waiting for a break in the traffic. Then Dorne could plant the charge without the danger that some teamster would light a cigar and drop a burning match that, conceivably, might accidentally ignite the fuse. A careful man was Mark Dorne, more particularly so now in his new hazardous occupation. He wanted no accidents, no innocent people hurt—his targets were very specific.

Haulage was always heavy with the slow-moving freight wagons drawn by long teams of mules or oxen, toiling up the west slope, over the crest to Strawberry, and down the eastern mountain face to the Carson Valley on their way to Washoe. Dorne had chosen this spot because most wagons stopped at the stage station to rest the animals, for teamsters to eat, leaving gaps in the endless procession. But today, for every string that pulled off the road, another left the station to take its place. And time was running out.

Dorne frowned at his watch. It was going to be close. Perhaps too close. He might have to abandon this attack, delay it another month. Then, as if the gods of justice smiled on him, three wagons in line turned into the station yard, and none left it. Carrying handfuls of the yellow sticks, he slipped off the hillside to where a small log bridge crossed a sparkling mountain stream. There, he capped the dynamite, placed it under the end of the bridge, fastened the fuse, and crossed the road, uncoiling the lethal line, kicking loose, gritty earth aside as he climbed back to his vantage point.

That there had been no uphill traffic for fifteen minutes warned The Major that the silver shipment was very near. For protection from road agents, the all-powerful company decreed that no freighters might drive within half a mile of the treasure train in the direction it was moving, and it was heavily guarded against the opposing traffic.

Dorne was barely settled when it appeared, crawling slowly up the stiff grade. As always, four mounted gunmen rode in advance, and the carriage behind them carried more as well—armed guards. The heavy silver wagon came next, and, behind it, another four horsemen brought up the rear. All the guards were hired killers, benevolently shielded from the law by the umbrella of Ralston's Ring.

The Major smiled. Not a pleasant smile. His practiced eye measured the speed of the advance and the distance of the train from the bridge. He knew precisely how much fuse he had unrolled, knew to the second how fast it would burn. It must not reach the charge neither too soon nor too late.

The train neared the bridge. The advanced outriders passed below him. The guard carriage moved into the target area. Dorne lit the fuse. Had one of the gunslingers glanced up, he would have seen a low plume of smoke lick down the mountainside, but all the attention was on the Strawberry yard where a freighter boss was just shouting his hitch back into the ribbon of dust.

The smoke plume snaked across the road, almost hidden by the grit, to reach the dynamite. The treasure wagon was on the bridge. It disintegrated. The air shuddered with the blast. The carriage of guards was close enough that it, too, blew apart.

Bodies, of men and horses, were hurled away by the concussion to become almost indistinguishable from the remnants of wagons and bridge. Two of the rear riders were killed and the other pair knocked from their saddles. Beyond reach of the rushing shock wall, the four horsemen in advance fared better, and turned their horses back toward the wreckage.

Dorne was on his feet, swinging the Greener on its swivel, first to pick off the survivors at the rear. He brought down one to sprawl in the road, and the other was spun and flung aside.

The Greener had been designed for goose hunting. The big Canadian birds flew at great heights, and these barrels were four inches longer than the longest shotgun in the country. Loaded with .50 caliber slugs, the weapon had a shocking power at two hundred yards. It could tear a man to bits. Dorne didn't hesitate to use it here. The men he fired on were jackals, murderers recruited from the slums of major cities and the outlaw gangs that prowled the West. He judged it was a service to the country to be rid of them.

He reloaded the Greener, and turned his attention to the advance riders who were now shooting at him. They were riding toward him, but had to haul up at the rim of the crater blown out of the road. Dorne turned the Greener toward them as one of the men yelled: "It's The Major. Get him. Sharon will pay ten thousand to the man who drops him."

Dorne shot him, then ducked behind the big tree trunk. It was not his intent to be killed by these hirelings. Not by anyone. He had a war to carry on. He stepped out to fire the second barrel, brought down another man, and moved back behind cover again, letting the Greener swing from his belt. He unslung the rifle, and with that he finished the remaining riders.

The panicked horses had bolted. Nothing moved on the road.

Freighters were erupting from the stage station, shouting, running toward the carnage. Dorne had no quarrel with them, but ten thousand was a tempting prize and one of them could kill him if he let them within range. He sent a burst of shots their way, but hitting short—a warning. They stopped. He ran easily along the hillside to the draw where he had four mules picketed, fitted with saddlebags.

He led them down to the road and picketed them close to the shattered wagon bed—they were spooked by the smell of blood. The freighters still stood in the stage yard. They were excited and curious about the blast and the massacre, but more approving than not, that so many of the hired guns were dead.

They watched, shading their eyes with their hands, while Mark Dorne pulled débris off the fifty-pound silver bars scattered in the dust and loaded two of them on each of the mules. That would be enough to finance him for a long while, buying time that he could spend chipping at the fortress of the ruthless Ralston Ring.

There were many bars he did not take, but he was sure not many of them would ever be retrieved for the Bank of California. The freighters knew what they were and how the ring operated. There would be a scramble, maybe some fighting about who claimed what, but these men had survived in this harsh country by guts and ingenuity. They'd find a way to hide some of the bars, maybe even find a method of cutting them into shares after a while, returning only a couple to the bank, letting it be assumed that the rest had gone with The Major.

Dorne pulled the pickets, caught up the lead rope to the mules, and turned toward the yard, swinging an arm in invitation to the men. There was a moment of surprised silence, and then a growing laugh.

Smiling, he started up the draw, leading the mules, and was out of sight by the time the freighters swarmed over the treasure.

Chapter Three

The magnets that drew the adventurous were gold and silver, wherever found. In particular, the wealth of the Comstock attracted a horde of hard-faced scavengers of a breed no less hungry for it than the Bank of California crowd who dressed in the disguise of gentlemen. Criminals gathered in Washoe from all across the world. Adolph Jinks was among those. Born in the slums of London, he had killed two men before he was eight years old. He had been caught and transported to the penal colony off the shore of Australia. At eighteen he had escaped, hardened by the years of association with the worst of society's rejects. Learning of the California gold rush, he had made his way to San Francisco.

He did not come to pan or mine the ore himself. He joined and soon became a leader of the notorious Hounds, a marauding gang that the Vigilance Committee finally drove out of the city. Jinks would have been hung, but again he escaped and found temporary safety in Placerville. When silver was identified on Sun Mountain, he moved east to the new territory and made a comfortable living holding up stagecoaches. Bill Sharon heard of his growing reputation, and, in a move to relieve the pressure on the coaches and at the same time make use of him, he offered Jinks the job of head security officer for Union Mining and Milling. He paid Jinks more than the man was taking at the point of his gun.

The day after Mark Dorne's attack on the silver bar shipment, Jinks stood with Sharon at the rotting scene. What could be found of the dead men and horses had been buried, or feasted on by birds and animals gorging themselves through the night, but a strong stench still pervaded the area from what was left over. The killer and the robber baron shared more than a lust for power. They were in a rage against one lone man.

"Damn him to hell!" Bill Sharon was a little man with dark, beady eyes and a cold, cruel temper that was most satisfied when he was breaking anyone who dared cross him. He squeezed the silver dollar medallion, left by Dorne and found by Jinks, as if it were The Major's neck he crushed. "He has to be stopped, and quickly."

"He will be." Jinks's voice was high, with a wicked rasp that was frightening in itself. "Dangler is coming with the dogs and fifty men. They should be here by noon, and we'll keep on his trail until we kill him or run him out of the country."

"Kill him. I don't want to hear of him coming back."

"It will be a pleasure. And I'll take my time, make it last. I want to hear the bastard scream his head off. I think I'll let the dogs have him."

Jinks untied his horse from the rear of the carriage they had driven up from Carson City, and Bill Sharon turned the carriage back down the grade. Jinks mounted and left the road, skirting the gaping hole, riding to the Strawberry station to wait where the air was less foul. He didn't want to miss a chance to frighten the stationkeeper enough to make him admit he had helped in the robbery, probably been paid with a silver bar.

Pete Dangler came with his posse. They took time for a quick meal, and at one o'clock they started up the draw where mule tracks indicated The Major had gone, the dogs held on leashes. They were especially trained mastiffs—big, powerful, and vicious—imported from England to run down thieves who tried to high-grade the Comstock mines. It is said a dog takes on characteristics from its master, and Pete Dangler had trained these to brutality and to obey only those people he trained with them. Dangler and Jinks had met at the penal colony on Van Deeman's Island, and the Britons had escaped together by murdering two guards and the crew of a fishing boat that had hauled them out of the water.

The fifty-two-man party climbed the draw, having trouble holding back the straining dogs, unaware they were being watched by Dorne. The Major stood on a shelf high on the mountainside where his strong field glasses brought the toll road close. He had witnessed Jinks's conversation with Sharon and, more recently, seen the wagons bring the men and dogs. The stop at Strawberry had given him the time to create a false trail. Intent on preventing those dogs from leading the search to the cave behind this shelf, he had spent the intervening hours preparing to mislead them.

He had dropped down the steep short cut to the valley where his mules were pastured, brought them to the trail where, yesterday, he had taken them to unload the silver. Then he retraced yesterday's tracks and scent, and returned in a wide swing in the direction opposite to the cave. This brought him to the valley bowl, saucer-shaped, probably a meteorite basin. It was surrounded by steep cliffs that could not be scaled. A water-carved passage at the lower end was the only entrance.

He picketed the animals inside, unwrapped the rope around his waist, tied a stone to one end, and tossed it over a pine bough that reached out from the rim fifty feet above the floor. When the rock came back down, he tied the ends of the rope together and pulled himself up, hand over hand. He left no track that the dogs could follow.

A superb athlete, Dorne could run a hundred yards in less than ten seconds. He had never seen a horse he could not ride. He had broad jumped a narrow cañon where a miss would have plummeted him a thousand feet to the rocky bottom. Climbing the rope was more play than work.

He had discovered the little bowl on his first survey trip to familiarize himself with the hills before he had begun his war and marked it as a trap into which he could lead an enemy. He had found the ledge and the cave behind it the same day. There was enough distance between the bowl and the cave to prevent the discovery of one as a lead-in to the other. He made it his headquarters. It was large, dry, comfortable. He had stocked it well with all he would need for an extended period. It was there that he manufactured his dynamite and there that the silver bars were stored until he was free to visit San Francisco and turn them into cash.

Now he waited on the ledge, with his secret preserved by the new scent trail, waited for them to turn up the draw from the road. He heard them before he saw them, bawling orders and cursing as they came.

Jinks had been at pains to change his speech and manners to conform to this new country and thus be less visible to those he wanted to avoid. His English was now close enough to the vernacular to pass. But Dangler remained a cockney bum, and his talk was all but unintelligible to American ears. He cursed his dogs in strange words and pushed forward in a careless hurry because Jinks had promised that, when Dorne was laid by his heels, half the reward would go to Dangler.

Seeing them reach the head of the draw, Dorne went into the cave to prepare for his next sortie. He put his buckskin jacket aside, and shrugged into a canvas vest. It was akin to the type worn by hunters, with rows of loops covering the front—meant to hold shells, but these loops were larger. They were meant for dynamite sticks, and he filled them. He left the Greener and the holster guns with their belt, taking only the rifle. He had to move quickly now.

He stepped out of the cave, paused for a look at the baying brutes that half dragged the men who held them. Then he left the shelf and ran lightly along the ridge to a point above the gateway into the bowl. He had not much more than reached it when the great dogs towed their handlers through it. Their hue and cry turned to vicious snarls at sight of the mules, and it was all the men could do to hold them from launching themselves at the animals.

In the lead, Dangler was yelling at Jinks: "Here! Al . . . the mules he used to haul the silver . . . the bars should be here somewhere. Now, all we got to do is run the bastard to ground."

Dorne was poised above them, his black clothes blending into the shadows under the trees. He waited until all members of the posse had moved through the narrow pass. He set a cap in one stick of dynamite, pressed in a short length of fuse, lit it, and tossed the bundle against the base of the far wall of the passageway. The explosion blew down tons of the rock into the gap and closed it with a fifty foot high barrier.

There was a paralyzed moment in the bowl, even the big dogs cowering on their haunches. Then the men were pivoting, scanning the bowl and the rim. Dorne was not in sight. By the time the echoes quit ringing from wall to wall, there was a rush toward the barrier. The men looked for escape. There was no escape.

"Dig . . . dig through!" Dangler was shouting as he ran, yanking the leashes from hand after hand.

Free of the dogs, the men clawed at the loose rubble, tried to climb the heap that slipped under their feet and rolled them back down.

Behind the tree that sheltered him, Mark Dorne set another cap and fuse, lit it, stepped out, and flung it down, toward Pete Dangler and the pack he held. His aim was true. The yellow death landed at the cockney's feet and sputtered toward explosion. The man saw it, screamed as he grabbed it to throw away from him. Too late. The blast went off in his hand. Man and dogs lifted into the air, torn apart.

The posse was panicked, running in circles, diving behind boulders that spotted the valley floor, unable to locate their attacker. Jinks had caught Dorne's movement as he threw the stick, had drawn his gun and snapped away a string of bullets, yelling: "There he is . . . shoot him . . . gun him down!"

Some of the men began firing at the rim, but their slugs only slammed into the big trunks of ponderosa. Dorne was behind one of those, preparing yet another charge. This one had Al Jinks's name on it, but when The Major put his head around the tree, he could not see his target in the second he dared risk exposing himself. He compromised, threw the stick toward the rock cluster where most of the firing was coming from, and ducked back.

The firing stopped when the stick exploded. Dorne stepped away from the tree, searching the bowl for Jinks. He had to go to the rim and look directly down to see his prey. Jinks was at the base of the wall, staring up it as if his eyes could carve a path to take him up.

For a second they looked into each other's faces, Jinks snarling as he swung his gun up and fired, but Dorne was gone before the bullet whistled past.

He was behind the tree, working deliberately, tying two sticks together, his hands shaking a trifle with the importance of this charge. Of all these hired guns, he wanted Adolph Jinks the most. It was Jinks who had ordered the strike breakers to attack the pickets at the Calico Mine. Jinks was the first to swing a club. Dorne did not know whether it was Jinks who had killed his father, but it did not matter. He bore the responsibility.

Dorne lit his fuse, stepped around the bole, and tossed his smoking package over the edge. He would have liked to have watched it drop, watch Jinks's body torn to shreds, but that would be a foolish exposure he could not afford. If he were shot at this early stage of his war, everything would be wasted. There was more at stake than a personal vendetta. His aim was to erode the forces of the barons who were grinding down the powerless—breaking their spirits, then hearts as well as bodies. No one else would champion the faceless, voiceless victims of the swine who swilled off the bounty of the country.

The rock under his feet trembled with the blast. For an instant he wondered if a fault in the cliff would fracture and slide the ground where he stood. At the bottom, there were still many guns trained against him. He jumped farther from the edge, running in plain sight for half a minute, and his luck held—no shots whined toward him.

He waited until the sound stopped slamming back and forth, until silence returned and he could hear whatever sound was made down below. When none came, he eased toward the edge again. There was a hole where Jinks had been, and the gunslingers were hugging the far wall of the bowl, their guns holstered and their hands stretched high over their heads.

Without leaders, they were not a force worth bothering with. Dorne's sights were on a higher goal. If he went away, they would eventually climb the barrier of rubble, straggle down to the toll road, and scatter into impotence.

The Major turned his back and walked away.

Chapter Four

On July 4th The Major walked into the Far West Saloon in San Francisco. It was two months since he had blown up the silver train at Strawberry, two months in which he had carried on his vendetta against the Bank of California. He had not been universally successful for he was finding that one man against the hundreds of employees of the powerful bank ring was simply not enough. He needed help, and there was only one man alive that he completely trusted, his former sergeant, Shawn Grogan. The trouble was that Shawn was still in the Army where he had another year and a half to serve.

However, Dorne had chanced seeing McEwan at the newspaper office. McEwan had agreed to contact Grogan, explain Dorne's need, and instruct the sergeant to secure a month's leave of absence and let Dorne know when he was coming. The Major had given the saloon as an address since he dared not approach the post offices either in Virginia City or Placerville. He was not wearing the black buckskins and cavalry hat used in his activities against the bank. It was the way the figure was dressed in the Wanted poster that hung in the post offices of Nevada and California. At present he wore civilian clothes and only a single gun at his hip. In this part of the country, no one had seen The Major in civvies, but he could hardly chance appearing as himself at the mint to cash in the silver bars. He needed Grogan for that. Dorne was not forgetting McEwan's list of volunteers, but both he and McEwan knew that, although this limited number of stalwart men could prove useful for gathering information and pos-

36

sibly supply safe haven when necessary, they didn't have the training or background for the job at hand.

The woman at the bar was wearing a red dress, and, even if it had not been months since he had been with a woman, he would have noticed her. She was worth noticing. There were empty places on either side of her. She seemed to be alone, and, from her appearance, Dorne judged that she had no business in a saloon.

The bartender was near the end of the bar. Dorne asked about his mail. When the bartender said there was no mail for a John Johns, the woman caught her breath audibly, and, when Dorne looked at her questioningly, she said: "Buy me a drink?"

There was a forlorn quality about her that stirred his sympathy. She must be new in this profession of women who haunted places like this. He really didn't want a drink, but neither did he want to hurt her with a refusal. He beckoned the bartender, waited until the bottle and glasses were before them. He poured two drinks, handed one to her, mustered a smile.

"You haven't worked here long, have you?"

Her chin went up in a defiant manner, but she looked at the retreating bartender before answering and kept her voice down. "I don't work here, Major."

"You know me?" He kept his tone low, appreciating that she realized he was using an assumed name for his mail.

She said: "I used to see you at Fort Lincoln. My husband was a sergeant in the Seventh."

Dorne had figured that sometime, somewhere he would run into someone who knew him, but he had hardly expected to run into a woman from the regiment in the Far West Saloon. He said, bluntly: "What are you doing here?"

"My husband is supposed to come in here. He left me

when his enlistment was up. I traced him to San Francisco and hired detectives to try and locate him."

Dorne made no comment, but the woman seemed bound to talk.

"I know I'm a fool, but I can't just give up without one more try to get him back. Thanks for the drink. I guess he's not coming tonight."

She put down the unfinished drink, turned, and moved toward the door. Dorne watched her, and suddenly stiffened. The batwing doors were slapped open by Shawn Grogan who stopped in surprise when he saw the woman. They stood for several minutes talking, then she nodded and went on out. Grogan came toward The Major.

Dorne was frowning. The sergeant was out of uniform. If he had been on full furlough, he would probably have been in uniform. Grogan was big, burly with an unruly shock of thick hair and a mountainous map of a face that could change on the instant from a devil-may-care joy in living to a lust for a fight. His eyes glowed with pleasure now as he took Dorne's outstretched hand.

Grogan's rush of words stopped Dorne's enquiry. "I almost didn't know you in civvies, and what have you done to your hair?"

Dorne shrugged it off. "It's part of a disguise. You'll hear it all. How much leave do you have?"

Grogan grinned. "None."

Dorne said: "I was afraid of that. You better head back for Lincoln as soon as you can get there."

Grogan shook his head. "I've had the Army, clear up to here." He held his hand above his head. "It's not the same with you gone."

"It's better than hanging, which is what will happen if they catch you."

"They won't catch me." Grogan reached for the bottle and the woman's glass. "No one knows me in San Francisco."

"That woman who just left apparently knew you."

The big sergeant tossed down a drink, and licked his lips. Dorne understood that the lick was a comment on the woman rather than the whisky, the sergeant's wink underscoring it. "Her? Mary Walters, sure. But she won't say anything to anyone. I told her that I've gone over the hill and to forget she's seen me."

The Major shrugged. "She knew me, too, although I don't recall ever seeing her."

"She was Duke Walters's wife, a good kid, but Duke was pretty much of a bum. He was in Myles Keogh's company. You probably never saw him . . . or not enough to remember." Grogan paused to take another drink, then grinned at Dorne. "And he'd better pray that she doesn't find him. He walked out, leaving her without a dime. The non-coms took up a collection to send her home to Ohio . . . instead she comes out here."

The Major had no real interest in Walters or his wife, but he was concerned about Grogan. Still, he knew the Irishman well enough not to waste time in fruitless argument.

Grogan snagged the bottle in one hand, took Dorne's arm in a vice grip with the other, and steered him toward a table that was being vacated.

"Hell, Major, we been there together, lots of times before, and, when you yell for help, I know you're there again. What's the score? What are we into now?"

Dorne had to laugh at the man. It was true that they had been out on a limb trying to cut through red tape in days past and so far had come through. He did need Grogan's solid courage and unflinching loyalty, and a man must make his own decisions. After he told Grogan what he planned, he would have Grogan's reaction and be able to judge whether to escort the man back to the fort in time to save him.

The Major outlined what he had been doing in a brief summary and watched Grogan change from shock and indignation at the Ralston Ring to a hearty enthusiasm. He finished by saying: "So, I've got a private war going on and a cave lined with silver bars but no money to operate on."

"Sounds like my kind of war. Can't you sell the bars to one of the banks?"

"The Bank of California crowd would see that we never got a dime."

"Then what do we do?"

"We take the silver bars to the mint. We fake a bill of lading from one of the mines, drive up to the delivery entrance of the mint, and trade the bars for dollars. That is, *you* drive up."

"It sounds simple."

"It is. The idea is to do things the obvious way because, if silver bars are stolen, no one expects them to show up at the mint."

"All right, where do we start?"

"We need a heavy wagon. I want you to catch tomorrow's stage over to Carson and buy a wagon and a six-horse team. Then I'll show you on the map how to find the cave where the silver bars are hidden. Drive up there. We'll load the bars. Then you drive back down here and deliver them to the mint."

Grogan nodded, grinning. They had another drink from the bottle, and then left the saloon separately. They met again on Market Street at the entrance to Dorne's hotel.

* * * * *

In the morning, Grogan caught the eastbound stage. The Major seldom rode public carriers and in any case had no desire to let anyone know of his and Grogan's connection. At least, not any sooner than necessary. He went down to the livery stable, had his horse saddled, and took the road for Placerville.

Three days later he was standing above the toll road, watching for Grogan.

The wagon finally appeared, pulling out of a line of motley vehicles and up the small side draw. They met at the head of the draw, tethered the team, and climbed to the shelf outside the cave. Grogan's reaction to the large, well-ordered space was surprise and admiration.

"This is some lay-out . . . and it looks like you could hold out here for a very long time. What's that?" Grogan pointed to a rocky shelf on which some dark-brownish fur was lying.

"I'll explain later, when I'm finishing it. First thing, we get the bars down to the wagon."

It took sweat and time to transport the bars from the cave to the nearest trail that would accommodate the wagon. This was just beyond the blocked passageway into the bowl. They bedded the load in the wagon and covered it with canvas. The team was secured and fed nearby.

Grogan stood looking down into the bowl. He indicated the mules below, no longer picketed. "What are you going to do with them? How you going to get them out of here?"

Dorne grinned. "Well, I blasted it closed before . . . guess I'll have to blow it open again to get them out. It'll have to wait. But they have plenty of fodder, and they sure aren't being overworked."

Back in the cave, having eaten, Dorne explained the fur.

"This hide is from a desert fox . . . I've only used the part which most resembles human hair. I dyed it . . . and it's about to become a better disguise."

"I think I saw your Wanted poster when I went after the team and wagon. I'm not sure I would have known you if McEwan hadn't said you were using disguises."

"Too many have seen that one now. I don't intend to wear another until after we've got the silver exchanged. That's why I want you to go to the mint."

Dorne picked up the swatch of fur. With patience, he pulled out the longer, stiffer hair, leaving the shorter under-matt, then used a straight razor to pare the skin to a thin supple lining. He cut gores, pulled the edges together with needle and thread to the shape of his head, a hood long enough to cover his hairline. With it on his head, he cut and fitted the beard down his cheeks, with a cup for his chin that would secure the whole wig and mask closely in place. It gave him a very different look—brownish in color and un-kempt. When the sewing was finished, he soaked the piece in water, put it on again, and wore it until it dried, shrinking to an exact fit.

It took until morning to dry, then he combed strands of his own head hair into the edges of the fur to cover the de-marcation line. Grogan had watched the whole proceeding the evening before, and he now shook his head admiringly.

"That dirty-brownish hair is blending right in. How'd you ever learn to make a mask like that?"

"Indians. A long time ago. Never thought I'd use it, though."

After a hearty breakfast, they hitched up the team, and Grogan pulled back onto the toll road and headed for San Francisco. Dorne would keep pace on horseback, not using the road, keeping to the solitude of the trees.

The mountains of the Sierra Nevada run high into the sky and are scored with deep, sharp cañons that drop to rushing waterways, impassable in the upper reaches except by bridges. Mark Dorne zigzagged down and up, coming into the open on the bridges and otherwise following animal trails, contacting the wagon at intervals to be sure Grogan was on schedule and had no trouble.

They met again in San Francisco for a rehearsal of Grogan's part, then separated. The sergeant drove on to the mint. Dorne's horse had thrown a shoe. He stopped at the blacksmith shop. They were to meet again at the livery.

That meeting did not take place.

The sergeant, dressed in a drover's clothes, arrived at the delivery entrance and hailed the man at the receiving door. The man stepped out, curious, asking what was wanted.

Grogan got down from the high seat, walked closer, and spoke in lowered tone. "I got a shipment here from the Ophir. Who unloads it?"

The receiver's eyebrows shot high on his forehead, and his words rushed out. "A shipment? In that? Where's the escort?"

Grogan gave him an exaggerated wink and grin. "New idea, to slip it through without that bastard blowing it to hell. Worked. Here's the bill of lading."

He handed over the fake bill of lading. The man indicated he should wait, and carried the document to the director of the mint. The director, Morrison, was not alone. Billy Ralston, the cashier of the Bank of California, had stopped by to take him to lunch.

The receiver repeated Grogan's story of the wagon's crossing the mountains unmolested. Morrison listened in astonishment, then smiled at Ralston.

"You don't get far ahead of Bill Sharon, ever. This is a slick one."

Ralston, who had been standing at the window looking out, turned. "What are you talking about?"

Morrison just handed him the bill of lading, still smiling in admiration. The banker took it and stared down at the figures that said the Ophir Mining Company was shipping fifty silver bars to the mint. He looked up, his expression grim.

"This is a fake, Morrison. Sharon might send the wagon that way, sure, but not without a duplicate bill of lading by messenger to advise the load was coming."

"Then who . . . ?" Morrison was genuinely puzzled.

Ralston shook his head. "I don't know, but I have a hunch that the shipper is the man they call The Major. Let's go talk to the wagon driver."

They went down to where Shawn Grogan waited impatiently beside the wagon, and they took three of the mint guards with them.

It was Ralston who asked the questions.

"You work for the Ophir?"

The sergeant looked from one to the other. He did not know what was wrong, but it was evident that something was.

He said: "Sure. Where do you think I got the silver?"

Ralston's voice was determined. "That's what I mean to find out." He turned to the guards. "Arrest this man."

Grogan stifled the urge to run for it. The guards all had guns in their hands, and he had no chance. It would be suicide to try, and to the pragmatic sergeant that would not help Major Dorne at all. He stood steady, looking as bewildered as he knew how, bluffing it through. His worst fear was that he would not be paid for the silver, that he would let The Major down, and his worry made the concern on his face genuine.

Then another guard appeared, and Grogan's heart sank. The man was Duke Walters, the husband of the girl, Mary, that he had last seen in the Far West Saloon.

Duke said: "Hello, Shawn."

Grogan managed a grin. "Well, Duke . . . I didn't know you were in this area."

Ralston swung around to Walters, "You know this man?"

"Sure. We were together in the Seventh Cavalry."

"When did he get out?"

Duke looked at Grogan. "That's a good question. When did you? The last I heard you had a couple more years to serve."

"Maybe he deserted." It was Ralston.

"That's just about what he did." Duke grinned at Ralston.

Grogan was filled with a feeling of hopelessness. He wondered what had happened to The Major. He had a vision of himself being court-martialed. He had no illusion of mercy from George Custer. The lieutenant colonel was not noted for mercy. But he kept an impassive face, and his eyes bored into the air above Ralston's head. A fatalist, as are most men who go often into battle, it was not his life that worried him, but that he had dismally failed The Major.

Ralston made a decision. "Look, we can find out easily enough. A telegram to Fort Lincoln will do the trick. So don't make the mistake of thinking that you can get away."

Grogan shrugged.

"Take him inside," Ralston told the guards. "Two of you unload the silver and take it to the vaults. You can credit it to the bank's account."

Morrison hesitated. Ralston was the most powerful man in California, probably one of the most powerful men in the world, but business was business. "Unless this man talks, how are you going to prove that the silver is yours . . . that it did not come from some other mine?"

Ralston reached in to turn over one of the bars. He indicated a tiny mark on the bottom of the bar. "Every bar that comes from one of our mines is marked. These bars belong to the bank, all right." Ralston was enjoying himself now. "Take this man to the office. Two of you stay and move the silver to the vaults."

Grogan was marched inside by Duke Walters, Ralston and Morrison trailing. Ralston took over the director's chair as a matter of course, leaning back to face Grogan across the wide desk.

He said, in a pleasant voice: "I've heard that they usually hang deserters?"

Grogan did not answer. His face remained calm. It was as if he had not even heard Ralston's words.

The banker waited a brief moment, then added: "So, I imagine you'd rather we not wire Fort Lincoln and let them know your whereabouts?"

Not a muscle or hair of the big man reacted. Grogan could have been carved in stone. Ralston appeared not to notice and went on silkily. "Well, you've got one chance. I know who you are working for. You are working for Major Dorne. Don't deny it. We know a great deal about The Major. We know that he was in the Seventh Cavalry. We know that he stole those bars from one of our treasure trains. We want him. We're going to get him with your help or without, so you need not feel guilty at shortening the search."

Grogan did not bat an eye, and Ralston's temper snapped.

"Damn it, I'm talking to you! Here's my offer." He slapped a hand on the desk top. "Lead my men to The Major and we'll say nothing about you to the Army. Instead, we'll give you ten thousand dollars in gold and get you safely out California. What do you think of that?"

Without moving his lips, Grogan's big voice growled: "I say it stinks."

Ralston sat back, regarding him wickedly, then said: "Too bad for you, then. The alternative is to lock you in the bank vault overnight, and tomorrow we will take you to Virginia City for further questioning."

Morrison lifted a brow, looking uneasy. "Why Virginia City? He could escape on the road."

"He will not escape." Ralston's voice was ice. "Because the bank owns that town. We are immune, whatever we do. I will have answers."

Chapter Five

Major Mark Dorne waited at the livery for Shawn Grogan to appear. He waited for the full afternoon. Then, worry tugging at him, he mounted his horse and rode to the mint.

The building was closed, but he had a view of a guard seated just inside the door. He rapped on the metal door with the butt of his gun until a second guard made his appearance. He slid back the small glass panel, saying angrily: "What's the matter? You drunk or something? The place is closed."

Dorne thrust his revolver almost into the man's face. "Come on, open up unless you want to lose an eye."

The man stared back, shocked speechless by the fact that this madman had the nerve to demand that a United States mint be held up.

Dorne read his thoughts. "This isn't a hold-up. A friend of mine brought in a load of silver bars this afternoon. He was supposed to meet me. He never showed up."

The guard said: "That must be the one the boys were talking about."

"And?" Dorne moved his gun suggestively.

"I wasn't here myself. I didn't come on duty until five, but they were talking about the guy who brought in a load of stolen silver bars and tried to sell them to the mint." He sounded a bit envious.

The Major's voice turned deadly. "What did they do with him?"

"I don't know. I told you that I wasn't here."

"Doesn't somebody here know?"

The guard turned his head. "You know, Jim?"

"No."

"They probably took him to jail. That would be the natural place to take him."

The Major said thanks. He swung around on his heel and went to his horse. He rode down to the city jail, tied the animal outside the shoddy building, and went inside.

There was a man on duty at the desk. He looked up as The Major came in and yawned: "What's your problem, bub?"

Dorne did not like being called that, especially by a redneck police sergeant. "I'm looking for a friend of mine."

The man looked him up and down from his flat-crowned hat to the fringed buckskin jacket. "What's his name?"

The Major hesitated. He doubted if Grogan would give his real name. "He's Irish, big . . . broken nose. . . ."

The sergeant held up one hand. "Save me the trouble of throwing you out, bub. You don't know his name. How am I supposed to find him?"

The Major remained patient. "All right . . . let me look in the cells."

"You've gotta nerve. Get out of here before I throw you in a cell and pitch the key away."

The next second the startled sergeant was staring down the barrel of The Major's gun. "Don't try to be funny. Just get up out of that chair and show me around."

The sergeant made a mistake. He tried to grab for the gun. Dorne bent the barrel across his head. The man went out like a snuffed candle.

Dorne stood, looking down at him for a full minute, then he went around the desk, took a ring of keys from a nail, and moved back to the grilled door that separated the block of cells from the booking office. He found the proper key, opened the door, and went through into a corridor with rows of cells on each side.

He stopped to peer into one cell after another. There were some twenty cells but no Grogan.

Disappointed, he turned and made his way back to the entrance. There he stopped. Four uniformed men had come into the room and discovered the unconscious sergeant.

They heard him and spun around. The leader wore a lieutenant's uniform.

"Hold up there."

The Major's gun was still in his hand. "Let's don't try and start anything, gentlemen."

The lieutenant swore. "Who in the hell are you?"

"Just a citizen who came in here looking for a missing friend. Your man here was very impolite . . . so . . . I had to clobber him."

The lieutenant jumped forward suddenly. The Major side-stepped and drove his fist into the man's stomach. The lieutenant doubled over in pain, and The Major chopped the back of his neck with the side of the hand that held his gun. The man went onto his face, unconscious.

Someone jumped on The Major's back and locked an arm around his throat, pulling his head backward. The Major relaxed his knees and let himself fall backward, pinning the man between him and the floor. He rolled as the man's grip was broken, put a knee into his groin. Then he came up, caught a swinging foot aimed at his side, and up-ended the man a second time.

The two who remained had backed away, drawing their guns. The Major reached inside his jacket and brought out a half stick of dynamite with a two-inch fuse. He deliberately struck a match and lit the fuse. The two men took one look, then fled, one by the door, one taking the window sash with him. The Major deliberately pinched out the fuse, stuffed the dynamite back in its place, and moved to the door. The two policemen were halfway down the block.

He moved out to his horse, mounted, and rode quickly in the opposite direction. But although he had routed the members of the law, he had not found Shawn Grogan, nor had he recovered the stolen silver bars.

"It looks," he muttered wryly to himself, "as if this round goes to the Bank of California."

What had happened to Shawn Grogan? There was no doubt that the guards at the mint had been telling the truth. Grogan had been arrested, but it was obvious that he had not been taken to the police station. Where then? Had he been turned over to the military authorities as a deserter? That seemed a logical possibility, but before he attacked the Presidio above the Golden Gate, he meant to check with the guards who had been on duty at the mint.

He rode back to the livery. The barn man was asleep in the office. Dorne did not disturb him. He unsaddled the horse, rubbed him down, and grained him. Then he found an empty box stall and curled up on a mound of hay, covering himself with his saddle blanket.

The Major was up at sunrise. He put on the wig mask. He left the horse in the livery corral, walked up Montgomery until he found a restaurant. Then, after his breakfast, he walked over to the mint and asked to see the director. He was sent to Morrison's office.

Once there, The Major calmly pulled out his half stick of dynamite and held it up. "Do you know what this is?"

The man's eyes bulged. "Who are you? What are you doing here?"

"The name," said The Major, "is of no importance.

What is important is that you and your people received fifty bars of silver from my man. The silver has not been paid for, and my man is missing."

"You're the one they call The Major."

"When they aren't using less courteous names, yes."

"Then you're a thief. You stole that silver."

The Major hesitated a moment, appreciating the director's fearless attitude. Then he said: "That is the bank's story. Mine is a little different. Let us say that they stole it from the earth, and I took it from them. I don't consider it stealing to take from thieves. I want the value of those silver bars in gold."

Morrison forced a laugh. His eyes were still on the stick of dynamite, but his voice was calm. "Not a chance."

"Then I'll blow this place up."

They stared at each other.

The director tried to laugh, but it didn't quite come off. His voice was still controlled. "You'll never get away with this."

"I am getting away with it," Dorne told him. "I'll take twenty pounds of gold coin. That should be about even."

The other shook his head. "I couldn't give it to you even if I wanted to. That money belongs to the bank and. . . ."

With his free hand The Major produced his gun. "I can shoot you, and then see if one of the guards has better sense than you do."

Morrison stared at him, ran the tip of his tongue around his lips nervously. Then he sighed and pressed a bell on his desk. They looked at each other without words until an assistant came to the door. The Major had thrust his gun out of sight. He could feel the stick of dynamite.

The director said flatly: "Lawrence, get four five-pound sacks of gold from the vault and put them in a bag."

The man showed no surprise. Much greater sums were handled as a commonplace in this building. Dorne might have demanded more except that a horse could carry only so much weight. Further, he had only sent Grogan with part of his silver cache and did not intend to rob from the United States Treasury.

Dorne waited until Lawrence had left. "Thank you. That's sensible."

The director sounded weary. "You'll hang for this. You're stealing government property."

"Bank of California property. Now, one thing more. What happened to the man who drove the silver wagon?"

"They arrested him."

"Don't lie to me. I searched the jail. He was not there."

"Mister Ralston had him taken down to be locked in the bank vault for the night. They were going to take him to Virginia City this morning."

"Why?"

The director shrugged. "He says they can handle things any way they want in Virginia City. Anyway, the man's apparently a deserter. One of our men recognized him."

"Why are you telling me all this?"

"I don't know. You're obviously intelligent and are probably usually reasonable. Yet this is stupid. You'll never get away with it."

Dorne thought he caught a note of regret and wondered momentarily what the director really thought of the bank ring.

Morrison would have said more but broke off as the assistant appeared in the door with a leather satchel, and handed it to him. He dismissed the man, opened the bag, showed The Major that it contained sacks of gleaming gold coins.

"You want to count them?"

The Major shook his head—negatively. "Let's go. You carry them."

"Where?"

"To the livery stable. You'll keep me company."

"What will I tell the guards at the door?"

"That you are going to the bank to deliver the payment for the silver bars to Ralston personally."

The other nodded, almost imperceptibly.

Dorne added: "Remember. I'm right with you, and this gun has a hair-trigger."

"And you'd get killed, too."

"Probably," said The Major. "A lot of people have been trying to kill me for some time. I'm sort of used to it."

With the mint director leading the way, carrying the leather bag, they left the building without incident and moved quickly along the street toward the livery. A different man was busy cleaning the corral at the rear of the building. Dorne appreciated the luck—he hadn't been wearing the wig mask when he left the horse. Dorne told the man he'd get his own horse and paid him. The man nodded.

Once in the barn, The Major secured the director's hands behind his back and prepared a gag for his mouth.

"I don't want to and can't shoot you without raising a ruckus. I'd prefer not to knock you out, so this should do if you'll be reasonable. That barn man will be finished in the corral and find you before too long. It'll give me a little time."

Then he saddled his horse, put the sacks of coins into his saddlebags, put the leather bag beside the director, swung into the saddle, and left.

He went quickly down the peninsula. With any luck the

barn man wouldn't find the director until he was well clear of town. He had one immediate plan. Get to the cave, leave most of the gold, and then push on to Virginia City to find Grogan.

Chapter Six

Although he had seen it many times, C Street at night was an experience that still amazed Mark Dorne. The crowded sidewalks, the permanently open saloons, and the constant flow of wagons seemed never to end.

Virginia City was built upon the most fabulous vein of silver that the world had ever seen. That wealth attracted all kinds of people and turned the barren slopes of Sun Mountain into a haunt for thieves and murderers and prostitutes.

More men were killed each day in the roaring town than anyone bothered to count. The most vicious of the mountain's murderers worked for Bill Sharon and the Bank of California.

For this reason The Major doubted that the sergeant would still be alive. He knew that Sharon would use any means to make Grogan talk, any form of torture conceivable, and he also knew that Grogan would not reveal a thing, no matter the torture.

How to find the man? The Major didn't think they'd have him in jail. Sharon might feel free to use any means he pleased, but he would not welcome outside attention. He had to find someone who might know where Grogan was being held. He expected to have to force co-operation in finding the hiding place. The question was—who?

His mind played with the idea of kidnapping Bill Sharon, but the man was always accompanied by three or four bodyguards, and he would be wasting time getting through them to Sharon. His mind flipped through the list of bank employees who might know where Grogan was hidden and came to rest on Paddy Gould.

Paddy ran the mills for Union Mining and Milling, and next to Sharon he was one of the most important men on the mountain. He lived in a large house down on the Carson River, near the largest of the mills.

The Major turned his horse, and rode down the twisting cañon past Gold Hill and Silver City, and on to the mill at Dayton. The thunder of the stamps was nearly deafening as he rode into the village.

But even the hammer of the stamps could not drown out the barking of the dogs. The Major had heard stories of these dogs that Gould used as guards for the mill's strong room. They were reported to have literally torn one man to pieces.

He stepped from the saddle, tied his horse to a convenient post, and moved toward the house that stood behind the mill. Gould, he thought, had to be deaf to live so close to such constantly jarring sound.

He reached the back door to the house and tried it, finding that it was locked. He used the bunch of skeleton keys that he always carried. He had to try a half dozen before he found the one that would work.

He eased the door open, finding himself in a big kitchen. There was a coffee pot bubbling on the stove, and he heard voices and the *clink* of cutlery from the next room. He peered around the edge of the doorjamb.

Paddy Gould and two other men were busy, eating dinner. None of them looked up as The Major loosened his gun and quietly stepped into the dining room.

Then Gould sensed his presence and looked around. He was a big, hearty Irishman with a walrus-like mustache and a whisky-burned face. His mouth dropped open with surprise.

"What the hell?"

The Major said pleasantly: "Don't anyone move, please. I'd hate to shoot a man just when he's full of dinner."

Gould's heavy mouth twisted. "Who are you?"

"I've been called a lot of things," Dorne told him. "Names don't matter."

"If you're here for silver. . . ."

"I'm not."

The man on the far side of the table stirred.

The Major swung the gun in his direction. "Don't move!"

A bullet crashed up through the table top and into the ceiling as the man fired from under the table's edge. The bullet passed so closely that it took a chunk out of Dorne's hat brim. Before the man could fire again, Dorne put a third eye in the middle of his forehead.

The man fell forward, burying his face in the mashed potatoes on his plate. There was a long moment of silence as all eyes fastened on the blood seeping into the potatoes.

Paddy Gould swore hoarsely. "I'll kill you for that. You just shot my brother."

"Too bad." The Major did not sound sorry. "He should have known better than to use a hold-out gun."

The other man at the table had turned a kind of bilious green. He gulped twice, then put down his head, and began to heave.

The Major stepped around the table. He patted his free hand over the man's pockets, not finding a gun.

"On your feet."

The man struggled to control himself. He rose slowly. There was what appeared to be a closet at one end of the room, with a key in the door. The Major retreated, keeping Gould covered. He pulled the closed door open, glanced inside. There was no other exit. "All right . . . inside!"

The man wavered a little as he moved, but he made the closet finally. The Major slammed the door, and turned the key. Gould was watching him, hate seeming to smoke from his blue eyes.

The Major said: "All right, whether you live or whether you join your brother in hell will depend on how quickly you can answer my questions. A couple of days ago a man brought a wagonload of silver bars to the San Francisco mint. He was arrested by the mint guards and turned over to Ralston. They held him overnight in the bank vault, and then brought him over here. I want to know where he is."

"Go to hell."

Dorne's move was lightning quick. The gun barrel shot out, raking across the man's nose, breaking it so that blood gushed down his shirt front. Gould cried out in involuntary pain.

"Damn you!"

Dorne hit him again, this time nearly tearing an ear from the side of his head, and then said: "I can keep this up longer than you can. Make it easy on yourself."

Gould was nearly sobbing. He said: "To hell with you."

The Major hit him a third time. He didn't want to knock the man out, but he meant to make him talk.

This time the striking gun barrel opened a cut under the right eye. Gould was sobbing now. He tried to bury his face in his crossed arms. The Major reached out, caught him by his heavy hair, and jerked his head backward.

"All right. Where have they put Grogan?"

Gould had had enough. Between sobs he gasped: "In the Lucky Boy Mine."

"Where abouts is it?"

"On the lower level. But you'll never get to him. They've got guards on each level just in case."

"That's my problem."

The Major started for the door and caught motion from the corner of his eye. Gould had ducked under the table, reaching for his dead brother's gun. He never managed to bring it up. The Major shot him twice, started out, and then deliberately moved back to unlock the closet. Without a further glance at Gould, he finally went out.

Outside, he paused long enough to get the wig mask from his saddlebags before mounting his horse and starting back up the cañon. Behind him, the stamps kept up their constant pounding. He thought about whom the bank would hire to run the mills now that Gould was dead.

It was nearly three in the morning by the time The Major rode the noisy length of C Street in Virginia City to the head frame of the Lucky Boy Mine. A burly guard stood in the rectangle of light, watching the rider pass, a hand resting on the butt of the gun at his side. The Major ignored him, continued on until he could no longer be seen, then dismounted and slipped into the dark and down the slope that dropped away from the road level. He made his way silently as the shadows engulfed him along the side of the tall, narrow building. There he climbed a trestle, in which hung the great pulleys and elevator cables, until he could jump to the peak of the high, steep, tin roof. Cat-like he landed with one foot on either pitch and, in the thick loose dust that coated everything, slid spread-eagled until his crotch touched the roof hip. Hunching along until he was at the front of the building, he leaned out to see where the guard was and found him directly below.

It was a long drop, but Dorne would have a cushion. He brushed sand away from the edge to give himself firm footing, drew a knife, planted his feet, and launched himself into space. He plummeted on top of the guard's back, drove him to the ground, locking his legs around the man's middle, and rolled with him out of the light. With the wind knocked out of him, the guard had no breath for a cry. Before he could draw in air, Dorne was astride him, slashing down, driving a knife blade deeply into the meaty chest. Then he rose and put an eye around the edge of the office window.

The mine worked only two shifts. There was no one in the room. Dorne surveyed the street, found it empty this far from mid-town, and dragged the guard along the building front to the corner and there tumbled him down the hillside. The guard's single heavy grunt had been the only sound.

Then he walked to the hoist. There was a two-compartment shaft, one for carrying the crew up and down, the other for lifting the ore and broken rock from the drifts far below ground. He chose the ore hoist. He stood there, waiting patiently until the rumble of the ascending hoist reached him. When the car, bobbing on its suspended cable, pulled level with the chute that would dump the ore into the wagons for transport to the distant mills, he was standing ready, waiting until the operator slid back the door.

The operator's eyes rounded until they looked like two fired agates as he saw the gun in The Major's steady hand. He choked. He had a prominent Adam's apple in a skinny neck.

"What . . . what . . . ?"

The Major said: "Don't yell. Run me down to the lowest level."

"But . . . but . . . I've got to unload this ore."

"Do it. I'll wait."

The operator hurried, his hands fumbling on the lever that activated the metal plate at the rear of the car to push the ore out into the chute.

Dorne said: "Relax. You won't be hurt if you behave."

The operator did not relax. He fought the lever, jammed the gears together, and the plate moved forward, dumping the load to spill down the iron slide. As he retracted the plate, Dorne stepped into the car just before it dropped. It fell with a speed that pumped his stomach up to his throat and stopped abruptly, dancing up and down at the end of the cable. The unexpected jar knocked Dorne to the floor. The operator ran out of the car and disappeared along the black drifts.

It was a mishap that could cost him dearly. The man would spread a warning to any miners who might be underground. There could be an army of hired killers looking for him soon. Dorne had hoped for time to search without being discovered but that was now denied him.

He stepped from the car, took a miner's lamp from the rack beside the shaft, and, lighting it, fastened it to his hat. Then he started along the drift the way the operator had gone. His gun was hanging loosely in his hand, and he stopped every few feet to listen.

He had traveled about a thousand feet when he came to a cross-cut and paused, debating which way to go. While he paused, a moving light appeared far down the cross-cut.

He doused his own so as not to warn the other and ran quickly and lightly, dragging one hand along the hot rock wall. This way he felt the wall turn and followed it and around another turn and found the open cave where an empty ore car could be sidetracked to allow a loaded one to pass. He stepped into it so that he would not be easily seen by the oncoming man, and waited.

The man was so close now that The Major could see the bony outlines of his face. He waited until the other had partly passed him before he suddenly shoved a knife against the man's ribs.

The miner swung a startled face. "What the hell?"

Dorne's voice was tight. "Over against the wall . . . face it. Put your hands out . . . rest your weight on them."

The man obeyed. Dorne used a free hand to run over him. The miner was not armed.

"All right, you can turn around."

The man turned. He stared at The Major with angry eyes. "Who in hell are you? What are you doing in the mine? You think I'm high-grading?"

The Major said: "No, my friend is a prisoner in this mine. I want him."

The man shrugged. "I don't know anything about it."

"Where would they hold him on this level?"

"I tell you I don't know nothing about it."

"But you do know the workings? There has to be a store-room for tools and equipment. Where?"

The man feigned stupidity, scratching his neck. Dorne put the sharp knife point under the chin and pressed until the head lifted.

"There is." He pointed the other way along the cross-cut. "It's down there."

"All right, show me."

The man hesitated, then, as the knife moved suggestively, he said: "All right. All right!" Turning, he led the way along the cross-cut until he finally reached a heavy plank door set in the wall of the tunnel.

There was a heavy lock on the door, and the Major said: "Open it."

"I haven't got the key."

The Major could have shot the thick padlock off, but he did not want the noise echoing through the tunnels. The hoist operator must have alerted someone by now, and a search was probably under way. Time was short, and, if Shawn Grogan were behind this door, it would be the first place they would come. He sheathed the knife, showed his gun, and said: "Sit down against the wall. I can draw faster than you can get up."

He picked the lock, then he kicked the door inward, calling, in a low tone: "Shawn, are you in here?"

A weak voice answered: "That I am, sir. What's left of me."

Dorne looked toward the miner. "Get up! Get him out!"

Fear had the man babbling: "I can't . . . his ankles are chained to the wall."

"I thought you didn't know anything about it."

The Major chopped the barrel of the gun alongside the man's head. The man fell down unconscious. He dragged the limp form into the room and kicked the door closed.

The room was far bigger than he had expected. Tools, shovels, single jack drills were heaped along the wall. Beyond them were stacks of powder kegs.

In one corner Shawn Grogan lay on a mound of dirty sacking. His feet were shackled to a ring of iron driven into the wall. His beard was matted with dirt, but it wasn't thick enough to hide the bruises where apparently he had been beaten around the head.

The Major swore under his breath. It was just one more score to settle with the bank crowd. The cuffs on each ankle had been riveted on. He found a drill and hammer with the other tools, but it would mean time and noise to drill out the pins and free Shawn of the cuffs. He set to work. When the last cuff was free, Grogan struggled up, first to his knees, then with the help of The Major's arm he gained his feet.

Dorne said: "We'll have to wait until later to get the cuffs off."

Grogan swayed back and forth for several minutes, then limped across and sat down on a powder keg. His face was greasy with sweat put there by pain, and The Major wondered if they would ever manage to make it out of the mine. He pulled a small bottle of whisky from his pocket and held it to Grogan's lips. The sergeant gulped greedily, then took the bottle from his lips, sighing gratefully.

"Brother, I needed that. Maybe now I'll live." His voice was gaining strength.

"Rough time?"

"Those bastards. I'll have their balls."

The Major knelt and tried to pound circulation into the sergeant's legs. After about ten minutes of this, Grogan rose and could take a dozen steps.

"It's all right. I guess maybe I can make it."

Dorne re-lit the lamp on his hat. He took the still lighted cap from the unconscious miner and put it on Grogan.

"Come on. We'd better get out of here as quickly as we can. The operator who brought me down got away. He'll let them know that we're somewhere in the mine."

He had brought an extra gun with him. He pulled it out and put it into Grogan's big hand. Then he put one arm around Grogan's waist and supported him to the door. There he stopped to put out the lamps before he opened it. Pitch black closed down, suffocating as a solid force.

"Do you remember the way they brought you in?"

"I never knew. I was out cold."

"Put your hand against the wall . . . we'll have to feel our way."

They moved slowly.

Dorne explained: "We're in a short drift on the bottom level, maybe about a half mile deep. Ahead there's a turn, and then about a thousand feet to the hoist. We'll be on top soon."

Letting Grogan guide them with a hand on the rough wall, Dorne half carried him, seeing nothing. A waft of air from the side told him when they reached the main tunnel. From there he counted the steps as he had automatically done on his inward trip. When they reached the hoist, the hot air funneled up in a draft. Dorne stopped, warned Grogan he must let go of him, then made a full circle of the place. There was no light in sight, and now he must be able to see. He lit a lamp, saw the shaft across the tunnel. But the car was not there.

He stood staring at the empty shaft for a long minute, then he crossed over and pulled the signal. They waited. There was no whir of machinery, no sound of the car descending. Nothing but silence.

The Major walked around the corner to the other shaft. He pulled that signal. Nothing happened. No sound broke the silence.

There was a trouble ladder bracketed up the shaft wall, but, weak as he was, Shawn Grogan could not possibly climb it all the way. Dorne went back to him.

"They're holding the lifts to bottle us up, Shawn. Now the signals have told them we're here. They'll be down in force. I'll get you up one level where they don't expect us."

Chapter Seven

The Major ripped the sleeves out of Grogan's bloody, ragged shirt and at the bottom of the ladder tied the sergeant's wrists to his own ankles and climbed. With his arms stretched over his head, Grogan fumbled his feet onto the rungs and pushed up with his legs while Dorne's legs pulled the bulk of his weight. Grogan grunted and sweat. Dorne could feel his trembling wrists through his boots, but the man kept moving.

It took time, precious time, and they could be caught midway by a dropping hoist loaded with guards. Rung by rung, they went up. It was thirty feet to the next level. They were within ten feet of the upper floor when Grogan's foot slipped off a rung. He jarred down, the other foot also giving way, and he hung over the void, suspended from Dorne's ankles.

"Easy," Dorne encouraged him. "I'll let down some while you find the rungs again."

"No use," Grogan's voice panted. "Legs are rubber. Won't hold me. Cut me loose, sir, and clear out while you can."

Mark Dorne did not even answer. Grogan weighed two hundred pounds in bone and hard muscle. Dorne's legs strained to lift the weight, wrapping his arms over the rung at his waist level, grappling both hands around one knee and raising that foot until it was solidly on the rung above. Then he brought up his other leg. In that fashion, he inched higher and higher, agonizingly slow, climbing against time.

When his head rose above the floor of the next level, he

stopped, looked along the tunnel, but there was no light, and he moved up again. Counting rungs, he stopped again, when the spacing told him Grogan's feet were above floor level.

"You're on top now, Shawn. Swing out to the side while I let you down. Get your feet on the ground, and just lean back from the shaft until you sit down."

Grogan kicked to the side of the ladder. It took three swings before he connected, and he grunted success when his feet held on the rock floor. Dorne eased back down, rung by rung, until all the drag against his legs was gone and the sergeant told him he was sitting safe. He then stepped off astride Grogan, and bent to cut the sleeves away. In the black hole they sat resting. Dorne forced the trembling out of his spent body, gaining control again. Soon, he was going to need it.

It was almost too soon. The hoist cable vibrated, machinery hummed, and the crew lift dropped past and bounced to a stop just below. It was an open lift, and Dorne looked down on seven little lights on caps and a blazing torch that thrust red glints from rifles already leveled on the lower floor by hard-faced men. If they had tumbled out of the car and gone searching along the drifts, they might have lived. Instead, one was shouting and pointing up the shaft. He had seen two men sitting on the upper floor as the torch momentarily had illumined them.

Now the guns swung up and a rattle of firing chattered like a cannonade as it crackled from wall to wall.

Dorne rolled back from the edge at the first volley, then looked down again, chose the man operating the lift and shot him through the head before he could start the car up again. Bullets whistled by Dorne. He ducked back and changed position, showing himself again, and dropped two more and became aware that Grogan had scrambled to the shaft and was firing. They had all the advantage on top, in complete darkness whereas those in the cage were caught in the torchlight.

Still, a lucky hit grazed the sergeant's arm, brought a gasp and a curse. The scene below was now shrouded by gunsmoke through which nothing could be seen except muzzle flashes. Dorne and Grogan aimed at those and were rewarded with yells as the lead went home. Abruptly the flashes stopped. Dorne could not tell whether all seven were dead, and he needed to know. Hidden by the smoke, he dropped down the ladder, not bothering with the rungs, slowing the fall only by catching one halfway down, then plummeting free.

He landed on a prone body, caught his balance, and groped through haze made dense by the red torchlight reflecting off smoke particles. His outstretched hand swept through the haze and touched the wool of a shirt. He closed his fingers on the cloth, and jerked the man toward him just as a gun he hadn't seen exploded almost in his face. Holding the shirt, he fired at it, heard a yell, and the weight of the body fell across his arm.

He dropped the man. He wasn't sure, but he thought this was the last man in the car. He backed against the rail of the cage to reload and wait for either further firing to give him a target or clearing air to let him see. There were no more shots. It was about five minutes before the smoke dissipated enough to show him the condition of the cage.

Five bodies lay on the car floor. The man he'd just shot was sprawled across two more on the rock outside. He called softly up to Grogan.

"All accounted for. I'll be up after a bit."

Noise of the battle would have funneled up the shaft,

and reinforcements would be gathering there to meet him when he and Grogan rode to the top. He needed a way to get past that force to the outside. He had dynamite, but the area up there was too small to use it. The head frame and the building would be blown down on top of them all. But the impenetrable smoke had showed him the way. Besides hiding the escape, it had the added value of fright. Fire in a mine was always a source of terror, and smoke billowing up the shaft would be translated as fire.

He caught up the guttering torch and ran for the store-room, broke open a keg, and filled the miner's cap with gunpowder, shoved that in a pocket, and snatched up the rags Grogan had lain on. The powder was not as effective as the new dynamite the mines were not yet using, but for his present purpose this was better. He jumped over the still unconscious miner and ran again to the hoist, threw the sacks into the cage, and lifted it to Grogan's level.

"Get in," he told Grogan. "Watch your step, it's slippery. Shove these bodies over the side while I get a surprise ready." Pleased that Grogan seemed a bit stronger, Dorne explained as he worked. "I'll use the torch to fire the sacking . . . fill this shaft so full of smoke nobody can see us when we hit the top. When we leave the car, I'll throw some gunpowder on the rags to flash up and fill the car with fire. I think they'll be too busy trying to kill that to give us a thought."

Grogan rolled the last body out to drop on the pile below it, sliding in the blood on the car floor.

"Half a mile up . . . how are we going to breathe?"

"Stay on your hands and knees in the corner away from the fire. The smoke will rise, fill the top of the shaft first, and hang under the roof. When we get up there, hold your breath and crawl out as soon as the car stops. Keep to your left and make for the entrance. My horse is tied below the mine dump. Head that way and I'll meet you there."

The sacks were damp, smoldering rather than blazing, belching smoke. Dorne took the car up slowly enough that the smoke was above them until they neared ground level.

"Now," Dorne said. "Hold your breath."

He sent the car up the final distance like a rocket. When it braked to an automatic stop, jouncing on the cable, they could not see but heard voices from the office. Grogan scrambled out of the car and out of sight.

Someone had heard the car and yelled: "Where's the fire? What level?"

Dorne called out, choking on the smoke: "Way down . . . bad!"

Stepping out of the car, he threw a capful of blasting powder on the torch, closing his eyes against the sudden bright flash. The lift blazed. The Major knew no one near would see anything at all for long minutes. He ran for the door, collided with someone, and slashed at him with his gun. He was lucky, catching the man in the head. Then Dorne was outside and running.

The air coming down the face of the mountain was cold and bracing. Dorne filled his lungs, and sprinted for the dump. Grogan was a dark, limping hulk ahead. They reached the horse together. The sergeant put a hand on the saddle horn, tried to mount, but didn't have the strength in his legs to get up.

"So damn weak . . . so damn weak," he was muttering.

Dorne laced his fingers into a stirrup, fitted it under Grogan's left foot, and boosted him until he threw the other leg across and dropped into the saddle. He led the animal at a jog. Just beyond the necklace of mines, he turned left at a corner, went down a cross street so steep it was built in steps. He turned again on B Street.

Grogan swayed, hanging onto the horn. "Where we headed, sir?"

"A bed for you at Julia Bulette's, queen of the mountain, the pride of the fire companies. She and her girls lead all their parades. She has the best house in town and doesn't allow rough stuff, not even profanity."

"Sir, she sounds just fine . . . but me, I ain't exactly in shape for them games."

"That's why we're going there. You're in no shape for anything, and Julia, among her other virtues, is mother and nurse to Virginia . . . and is discretion itself. I want you safe while you heal."

Grogan was so near fainting that he didn't make his usual protests about being able to take care of himself.

Dorne led the horse downhill again to the barn, behind and a full story lower than the house. He helped the sergeant dismount and go up the rear steps. He was one whom Julia trusted with a key to that back door. Now he opened it, and walked Grogan into the kitchen.

The night was almost gone. There was light in the east, and Julia sat alone with a cup of coffee and a brandy bottle, cooling out after the busy hours. She came to her feet, frowning at the stranger coming in, then saw Dorne behind him as he shucked off the wig mask. She did a double take with a quick smile, then indicated Grogan.

"Mark! What in God's name happened to him?"

"Sharon. His muscle boys asked him where to find me."

She moved quickly, turned a chair, and shoved the brandy across the table. "Sit him here and give him a drink while I get some hot water in the tub."

Dorne got the sergeant seated, put the bottle in his hand, and knelt to take off the boots, then peeled away what was left of the shirt. They heard Julia in the laundry room, pouring steaming water from the stove reservoir into the tin bathtub. When it was half full, she came back to them, issuing orders like a drill sergeant.

"Stand him up, Mark, while I pull those pants off."

When the sergeant stood naked, she made indignant sounds at the raised red welts and darkening bruises covering his body. She took one elbow and Dorne the other, and they steered Grogan to the tub. Between them, they got him into it. It was too short for him to lie down, and he sat, knees bent, leaning on them while she dipped a sponge and squeezed it over his head, softening the dried blood before she gently mopped it out of the hair, talking soothingly as she would to a child.

"I have a downstairs room for you just off the kitchen. We'll have you in some clean sheets right away, and sleep is potent medicine. Damn Sharon to hell!"

"I'll double that," Grogan said in a exhausted voice. "But, ma'am, first could I have a bite of food? It's seems a week since I ate."

"Animals! Beasts! Mark, you finish him here while I get a robe and start breakfast. How long is it since you've eaten?"

With the pressure of the search and rescue off, Mark Dorne was suddenly aware of his own ravenous appetite. He gave her a warm smile, rare for him in these days, and told her: "I could use about a side of ham and a dozen eggs, Julia. This war burns up energy fast."

She left them, and came back shortly with a robe, feminine and frilly, and a home-concocted salve, black and noxious but soothing as she spread it thinly over Grogan's cuts and abrasions. Then she went to make breakfast for all of them.

Finally Grogan was full, but silent in embarrassment at wearing the perfumed garment. Julia laced his coffee heavily with more brandy, and they were rising to take him to the bed when noise on the porch stopped her halfway out of her chair, made her hiss: "Could they have followed you?"

Dorne was on his feet, snatching up the wig, taking Grogan's arm to hurry him out, but it was too late. The rear door banged open, and a tall, powerful figure burst in, his big voice filling the kitchen.

"Julia . . . fire in the Lucky Boy. Are any of my men here?"

"Tom! No . . . none. Mark, this is Tom Peasley, the Volunteer Fire Department. Tom, do you know Major Dorne?"

Chapter Eight

Mark Dorne knew Peasley by reputation as one of the most noted gunmen on the Comstock and a man who had no use for Sharon or the bank ring. His life was wrapped up in his beloved fire department. He barely nodded to The Major, took a quick, bewildered glance at Grogan in Julia's flowing robe, then flung back toward the door.

Dorne's laughter spun him around, his jaw thrust out belligerently, and he roared: "Fire in a mine is not funny, you, whoever you are, it's a killer!"

"Real ones . . . but this one is a fake, Peasley. Let me tell you about it."

He made it brief, watching Peasley's expression change from anger to astonishment, then recognition and a grin as he put out a hand.

"The Major, huh? I didn't pay attention. I like your guts and what you're doing. But you're going to get yourself killed. That crowd's too much for one man."

Dorne shook Peasley's outstretched hand, liking the hard, assured grip. "I expect it to be," he said simply. "But while my luck holds, I mean to hurt them where I can. I don't like what they did to my parents and those miners. I don't like what they did to Grogan. Look."

The sergeant was glad to take off the robe at Dorne's gesture. Peasley walked around him, looking at the battered body, his face a thundercloud.

"God . . . and cuffs riveted on you." Peasley sounded sick at the pain for Grogan. "Go to bed, man, you need to rest."

Grogan staggered as he started to walk. Julia and Dorne, one on each side, steered him out of the kitchen and to the room and bed she had prepared. He was asleep before they left the room.

They returned to the kitchen where Peasley was pouring coffee for the three of them. Peasley was gruff with an emotion he seldom showed, saying: "Major, I understand your fight, and you're good for the camp's morale. Everybody's laughing about the freight wagons at Strawberry. I hear they're making bets on who's going to retire with a silver bar or two. The miners . . . three-and-a-half dollars a day boys . . . haven't any sympathy with the ring that's squeezing them, and you're squeezing the ring. Did you know they've kicked up the price on your head to twenty-five thousand? They can buy a lot of help getting you for that kind of money. But you're making a lot of secret friends, too. I wish I could help. I hope you survive."

Dorne smiled, relaxing in the warm kitchen and the company of these people. It was good to feel among friends, to let down his guard for a little respite. It was the first such moment he'd had since he had looked on his father's body and into his mother's empty eyes. But soon he would be out again, with Grogan he hoped, on his one-sided campaign.

Peasley's mind was still on the ring and its ruthless use of power. "You know what they're up to now? Know this Prussian cigar maker, Sutro, who had the gall to open a mill independent of the combine? He's promoting a good idea, and they're after his scalp for it."

"What idea is that?" It had been at least a year since Dorne had been in Virginia City and he knew nothing about Sutro.

Peasley went at it obliquely. "You know the condition in some of the deeper mines, they're into hot water, so hot a man can't touch a piece of ore bare-handed. Fortunate for your sergeant the Lucky Boy isn't down that far yet. Now Sutro, with his mill down below on the river, got to thinking how the miners work . . . hoist the ore all the way up to the surface, then haul it all the way down to the river. He says a tunnel ought to be driven from river level into the foot of the mountain, hooked into all the mines, for three purposes. It would make a haulage way, ventilate the mines by draining the poison air through a cross shaft, and he wants a channel in the floor to take out the boiling water and make the low levels fit to work in."

The picture was clear and reasonable. Dorne said: "Sounds fine. So he's an engineer?"

"He isn't. Just got a head on his shoulders."

"Cost a lot to build. How is he financing it? Where's his profit?"

"A tax on the ore a mine ships and a fee for taking out waste rock. That's why the ring is against him. First they didn't oppose him, then they sharpened their pencils and figured what it would cost the mines, how much the tunnel would earn at their expense, and they set up a howl. They're calling him Crazy Adolf. Tried to get Congress to revoke his charter, and, when that didn't work, they blocked him from financing through American banks. He went to Europe for money, and they beat him there. But they haven't stopped him from trying."

Dorne perceived the possibility of a common cause with the Prussian, was sympathetic with the stubbornness of the man, and felt a strong urge to have a hand in the project. If the tunnel could be built, it would be good for the miners and another way to strike at the pocketbooks of Ralston's Ring. He said softly: "He sounds like my kind. I want to meet him."

Julia said eagerly: "The miners swear by him, Mark. Tom, you can arrange a meeting with him." She turned again to Dorne. "Mark, he's just back from Europe and staying at the International."

While they had talked, the day had become full. Tom Peasley pushed up with restless energy. "I'll set it up. Where do I reach you?"

Julia answered for Dorne. "Right here. His eyes look like he's bleeding to death and the black circles are like targets. Mark, you can't go twenty-four hours every day."

"That's horse sense." He gave her a wry smile. He was bone tired with no rest since he had left the cave.

Peasley left. Julia showed Dorne a room, was starting to leave when she saw the wig mask where he had put it on the night stand. She picked it up and paused in the doorway.

"Looks like it could use a little expert attention." She grinned and, signaling good bye, was out the door, closing it behind her.

Dorne slept longer than he intended but awoke snapped back to resilient readiness. When he appeared in the kitchen, Julia was there. She held up his wig mask.

"I hope you like the color . . . I used henna . . . red hair should suit you very well."

"Why?"

"After what you did yesterday and last night wearing this get-up, I figured you needed a change. A lot of people saw you and by now they're talking."

Dorne laughed. "You're right. I don't usually forget about details like that."

"Trouble is, it's not dry, and it needs to be. I thought you could borrow one if you don't mind."

He raised an eyebrow. "Borrow?"

She reached into a basket beside her and produced a straight-haired, brown-black wig. "One of my girls used it playing a man's part in one of our entertainments. She's a good-sized woman. This should fit."

Dorne grinned, sat at the table, and allowed her to put the wig on and hand him a mirror. "What part," he asked, "a page at the king's court?"

"Sort of . . . but you won't have a beard."

He considered his mirrored image, this time seriously. "Maybe I could use one with this type of hair. Nothing I've worn so far is anything like it. Too bad I didn't grow a mustache. But there aren't many who have seen me bare-faced."

"Try a hat with it. And there's a jacket . . . one of my clients left it." She hurried out of the room but reappeared almost immediately carrying a Levi's jacket and a hat.

He shrugged into it, looked at her questioningly.

She nodded. "It's a bit large . . . that's good, makes you seem a little shorter."

When Peasley came for him, he was seated at the table wearing the new get-up. Peasley glanced at him, and then looked around inquiringly.

"It's me." Dorne laughed at Peasley's questioning look. "I'd just as soon not be recognized here in town with all Sharon's men around."

They left by the rear door, climbed the cross street where a "thank you ma'am" every two feet corrugated the road. They took C Street north to the hotel. The crowds on the sidewalk greeted Peasley with smiles and comments but had no interest in the man beside him. They climbed the wide central stairs to the third floor, and Peasley knocked on the white door of the corner suite.

A man of early middle age with the beginning of a paunch, bushy sideburns and hair already receding from a domed forehead, and a slightly hooked straight nose opened to them. Heavy eyelids made Sutro appear to squint as he inspected the man he was expecting, then went wide when Mark walked in, took off his hat, and mask. Peasley chuckled at the reaction, closed the door behind him, saying: "Major Mark Dorne, Adolf. He's as fond of Bill Sharon as you are."

Sutro gave a guttural growl. "I told Tom earlier, Major, the ring had word all over Europe . . . lies about me . . . turning the bankers against me. I couldn't move without their lawyers dogging me."

Dorne's tight mouth lifted at one corner. "It isn't lawyers they send after me."

"So I understand. Tom has told me of your action last night. I am glad to report a letter I received in England says you have the ring hysterical."

"Not yet, but they're getting uncomfortable."

"Good . . . good. Keep it up."

"I intend to, but with their control of mines, water companies, timber grants, every time I take twenty thousand from them, they've made another million."

"And are greedy for more. Always more. They try to stop my tunnel, but they will not. I go next to the miners, Major."

"Why? At three fifty or four dollars a day they can't raise enough to finance you."

"*Ach*," Sutro disagreed. "There are many of them, and they are angry. My tunnel will make their lives much easier and safer. When there are fires down below, it will let them escape. They are behind me strong. You will see if you come to our meeting at Piper's Opera House."

"Glad to. Mister Sutro, I'm here to offer any help I can give."

Dorne admired the indomitable will of the promoter. He and Peasley left. Dorne needed to make a stop at a store suggested by Sutro. Grogan needed new clothes, and The Major needed a new hat. Peasley went off on his own business

At Julia's, Dorne found Grogan still weak but gaining. He was glad to see the new clothes and wanted to put them on immediately.

At dark, a throng gathered at the ornate Opera House above the business district at the corner of Union and B Street. They filled the thousand seats and the standing room. Those who could not crowd in stood outside under the open windows. Major Dorne was in the front row beneath the speaker's stand.

Sutro was eloquent, a strong salesman extolling the virtues of the tunnel and spicing that with stories of the ring's efforts to deny its comforts to the men. When he had them spellbound, he asked that everyone present buy as much stock in the tunnel as they could manage. There was a lag, and Dorne stood up. It was a risk, but the disguise had succeeded so far.

"I'll buy a thousand worth."

He said it loud enough to override the talk beginning in the big room. Then he jumped to the stage and put a heavy bag in Sutro's hand. Sutro opened it and shook gold coins into his hand and then gestured with it.

"A thousand gold dollars, friends . . . who will be next?"

There was a concerted rising, a yelling of enthusiasm, and a crush forward. Among them, Dorne saw many with short clubs bulling through—toughs hired to break up the meeting. Fights were beginning. If, in a mêlée, Adolf Sutro was trampled under, there would be no tears from the ring.

81

In seconds, the big crowd would explode. Mark Dorne took Sutro's arm to pull him back, but the man stood firm with stubborn courage.

"Let's go," Dorne urged. "This is planned. They'll kill you."

A brutal-faced man jumped to the stage, swinging the loaded end of a billiard cue, aiming at the tunnel man. Dorne shot him just before he reached Sutro. He grabbed Sutro, and hustled him behind the stage curtain, through the short alley of dressing rooms toward the door to Union Street. As they went, Dorne yanked off the wig, stuffed it in the roomy pocket of the jacket. They were barely out the door when a gun exploded, spattering lead against the theater wall.

Dorne fanned his gun in return, stopping the rush, telling Sutro: "Run. I'll hold them."

The Prussian turned up the hill, but was unable to run the steep grade. Dorne did not look after him. He dropped the gun in his holster. As the charge came on again, he opened his coat, reached for dynamite in his vest, capped and fused it, and lit the short length. Bullets reached for him. He threw the stick just short of the man in the lead. The explosion tore him apart. Three behind him also fell, lay still, their clothes smoking, then breaking into flame.

The others braked their rush as they saw Dorne bring out another stick. They turned and dashed off downhill. He didn't know if they had time or light enough to connect his appearance with that of the man on stage in the wig. He found he didn't care. Let them recognize him and remember. He welcomed it.

When they disappeared around the first downhill corner, he jogged up to Sutro who was just reaching A Street and blowing heavily. Dorne slowed to the man's pace as they climbed on toward Howard Street and the mountain beyond. Sutro managed the breath to gasp: "The explosion, what was it?"

"Dynamite," The Major said.

Sutro looked over his shoulder, saw no one pursuing them, and stopped, sounding excited: "You mean the stuff Nobel makes in Sweden?"

"That's right. Keep going."

Sutro began moving again. "But where did you get it?"

"I make it."

"Here in Nevada you make it?" He was quiet until they made the upper street, then he said: "Major Dorne, I will remember that when I begin my tunnel. I'll give you a market for all you can produce."

Chapter Nine

Mark Dorne, one arm stretched behind him to help the laboring Sutro up the hill, smiled appreciatively. Even as this man extended all his physical strength to this narrow escape, he had time to latch onto an idea that would speed the work on his tunnel. A single-minded soul, Adolf Sutro.

At the corner of Howard Street, Sutro stopped, sucking noisy breaths, needing rest, looking down the way they had come. The Opera House rang with yells, and outside a mob was milling, fighting with clubs and fists.

"You're right," Sutro panted. "That was Sharon's doing. They've tried everything else, now I think he wants me dead. Major, where are you taking us?"

"I was recognized when I used the dynamite," Dorne told him. "They'll search the town for me, and, if they find you with me, you won't be safe. There's an old prospect hole a little farther up where we can wait until things cool off some. Let's get out of sight."

They moved on again past the last straggling building, onto the dark flank of Sun Mountain, up an animal trace. Every inch of that hillside had been scoured by prospectors, and it was pocked with diggings that had disappointed those in search of ore. The one Dorne chose was shallow, perhaps five feet deep, and wide enough that they could sit in it comfortably.

He probed with a stick to be sure there were no snakes in the bottom, then dropped into it, and gave Sutro a hand down. There was no moon, but the desert sky was made chalk-colored by brilliant stars, and the wind that usually blasted across the slopes was barely a breeze. Sutro sank against the wall sighing, his tired voice a hoarse whisper.

"Do you think they'll come up here tonight? If they wait for daylight, they can see us from above."

"We won't be here then." Dorne chuckled. "We'll give them the night to turn Virginia inside out, then before daylight we'll drift north, go down behind the hotel, and slip you into your suite."

"So," Sutro said in a bitter tone, "I must hide in a burrow like a jack rabbit now. And if I get to the hotel, then what? I cannot raise money and build a tunnel if I cannot walk on the streets. I am not afraid to die but, *ach,* dead I could not do anything at all. The swine!"

"There's a way to tie their hands, I think. When we get you to the hotel, send a note to the *Territorial Enterprise.* Ask Arthur McEwan to come to you and tell him what was tried. Tell him I back up the story. He'll spread it over the front page, and it will be picked up across the country. With that kind of exposure, the ring won't dare touch you personally. Even if you had a genuine accident, they'd be accused of murder, and, big as they are, they probably couldn't beat that. Too many people want you to build your tunnel. You'll be all right when the paper comes out. Just for good luck, let a couple of Peasley's men stand guard until then."

"Fine. Fine. You have a good head. *Ach,* I would like to see their faces when they read. And it will be my first victory against them. Well, should I take the first watch?"

Dorne's respect for Sutro was raised another notch. The man hadn't really regained his breath, the brush with death had not fazed him, and, exhausted as he was, he made this offer. But The Major could not risk that Sutro would fall asleep or miss some warning sound.

"I'll take it. You sleep," he said.

Almost at once, Sutro was asleep. Dorne settled back, relaxing, his eyes on the stars, resting but alert. He did not wake Sutro until the sky began to pale, then spoke his name softly, twice, before the man roused. They climbed out of the hole, and worked across the flank of the slope, Dorne studying every shadow, every movement of a night animal as it hurried away from the man smell.

Above the hotel they turned down, crossed B Street, and were near the rear door when they surprised a scavenging dog that sent up a frantic yelping. Immediately feet pounded behind them, and five men turned the corner of the building, loping toward them.

"Run," Dorne ordered. "Get inside. I'll stop this."

Sutro ran as The Major faced the new threat, reaching for dynamite. He lit it, held it to be sure it was burning, and threw it at the feet of the running men. But the dog scudded past him, the stick hit its back and deflected up. Instinctively the front man caught it, realized what it was, and hurled it back toward Dorne.

Dorne saw it coming, knew there was not time for another stick, turned and sprinted away, but the dynamite exploded in the air, and concussion knocked him flat and stunned him. He lay unable to move, groggy. Before his head cleared, the five were on him.

Two grabbed each arm, yanking him upright. He wrenched, kicked, his head ringing, but they held him fast. The leader, evil-faced, pig-eyed, showed a snaggle of broken yellow teeth in triumph.

"Got you. All twenty-five thousand bucks worth of you, Major, and you're a dead man right now."

"Not yet," another said hurriedly. "Bill Sharon would rather have him alive, more information to get out of him

. . . where's all the loot he took?"

"Sharon's in Gold Hill, so what do we do with The Major?"

"Jail, of course. He's a killer, ain't he? Let the law swing him."

The leader chopped his gun sidewise against Dorne's temple, and The Major went limp.

That was the last he knew until the jar of landing on the floor of a cell waked him. He had no memory of being dragged through back ways to the courthouse without being seen.

He lay on his face, limp, orienting himself. He heard vicious laughter, heard the grille clanged shut and locked, then the tramp of boots going away down the corridor. The stench of previous occupants was strong. When his head stopped reeling and his senses told him he was alone, he opened his eyes, and rolled to look around him. There was a narrow cot with a thin straw mattress and a folded blanket, a slop bucket, and nothing else.

Taking stock, he learned that his coat and vest were gone, his belt, guns, and knives. He sat up, doubling his knees, and felt under them through the fabric of his pants. A grim smile stretched his mouth to a thin line.

"Turnkey!" He called it loud enough to reach the office.

A man, sleepy from all night duty, came down the hall, stopped before the grille, his mouth wide in a yawn that ended on a grunted: "Yeah?"

Mark Dorne was on his feet, leaning against the bars, holding a ten dollar gold piece. The jailer's eyes rounded.

"Where'd you get that?"

Dorne smiled, sharing a joke. "In my boot heel. Take it, buy me six cigars, and keep the change."

The man took the coin, returning the smile, having a joke of his own. "Right, Major, that's mighty generous. But I'd say six is too many for you."

"Why?" Dorne pretended innocent surprise.

"I don't expect they're going to leave you alive long enough to smoke that many."

"That so?" The Major did not sound concerned. "Tell you what, you bring them anyway, and, if I'm hanged before I've used the lot, I *will* what's left to you."

The man shook his head slowly, chuckling appreciatively. "You know, Major, I've had a secret admiration for you . . . not that I'd let you escape, of course . . . and I've got more now. Here you are, knowing you're going to die, and you got the guts to stand there cracking jokes. I'll hate to see you go."

He flipped the coin, caught it, and went, whistling, on the errand. Dorne sat on the cot, his eyes closed, willing the headache to lessen. Before he thought the jailer had time to be back, there were sounds in the corridor, and, when he looked out, William Sharon was there with three of his bully boys. Sharon stood gloating, but his voice had a ring of wonderment under its chill.

"The Major. Caught. How one lone man could raise the hell you have escapes me, but that's finished now. Stand up."

Dorne watched him in silent scorn, not moving.

The icy voice repeated: "Stand up when I tell you to."

Mark Dorne sat rock still, his eyes boldly on Sharon's until Sharon flushed a dull red and flung around, snapping his fingers to the men behind him.

"Bring the key. Go in and stand him up."

All three went into the cell and stood over Dorne, one growling: "You heard Mister Sharon. On your feet."

Dorne sat, still watching Sharon—the head of the ring, his contempt too obvious to be missed. A blackjack swung against his head, knocked him to the floor. He was yanked upright by his collar and held while the other two pounded him. A grunting, panting voice grated,

"Last night, you blasted two good friends. Show some fight . . . make me kill you . . . just make me." Sharon's words bit at The Major. Then: "Enough! Stop! I want him to hang in broad daylight in front of the whole town. I want him in shape to know it."

The man holding him up opened his hand, and Dorne crumpled. He lay where he dropped, hearing the men tramp out, lock the grille, and parade with Sharon out of the jail. One eye was swelling shut, and his stomach churned.

He was still on the floor when the jailer brought the cigars, then he dragged himself up, leaning against the grille, half smiling at the astonished face outside, knowing that his own was lumpy with bloody bruises.

"At least you're alive. I saw Sharon and his bully boys leaving as I came back. Thank God they didn't see me."

The man proffered the cigars, and Dorne took them. "Matches?" he queried—knowing the answer.

"Prisoners ain't allowed matches, but I'll light you when you're ready."

"Now."

The jailer held a match until the cigar was glowing smoothly, then went away. Dorne lay on the cot, methodically relaxing, gathering himself, waiting for strength to make the next move. In half an hour he was ready, had lit a second smoke from the first, and got up to test his legs. There was still some tremble in them, but he could not wait longer. The morning was going. The court would be convened.

There were two empty cells across the corridor, and only by pressing his face against the grille could he see into the front office. The guard had changed, and a new man sat at the desk with a newspaper. Dorne retreated to the far corner of the cell and pulled up a pants leg. Behind each knee a short length of dynamite, capped and fused, was taped. The time to use one reserve was now.

Chapter Ten

The Major drew on the cigar, held the fuse of one stick against it, and, when it sputtered, laid it on the floor under the door, went again to the corner, and took the cot and blanket and crouched behind this ready-made barrier. It was little shelter, but the charge was not heavy. With his back to the wall and his head tucked down, he counted.

On time the explosion came. The cell filled with the sharp, acrid odor of burnt cordite. Before the echo died, Dorne was up, running, seeing with satisfaction that the lock was shattered. He kicked the grille open and sprinted for the office. Halfway there he met the new jailer running toward him. The man braked, making a grab for the prisoner. Dorne raised the second stick, holding the cigar close to the fuse, thrusting it toward the man's face, and yelled a sound of warning.

The jailer's yell matched Dorne's. He spun and dived for the outside door. Dorne had only what time it would take for the man to recover his wits and give the alarm. He found his vest and the coat borrowed from Julia and shrugged into them while searching the desk drawer for his guns and knives. Julia's wig was crumpled into one of the coat pockets. He tugged it on, considering the rumpled look to be an advantage at the moment.

Feeling dressed again, Major Mark Dorne walked out of the courthouse.

He took the grade in long strides that ate ground. None of the few people on the side street more than glanced at him. At the corner of C, he looked both ways along the sidewalk that was crowded there, attracting no interest. He dodged between two loaded ore wagons. Behind him somewhere, a roar of consternation rose. The jailer had broken the news that The Major was loose.

At D the traffic was light. Most of the businesses on the lower street were cribs, and this time of day the girls were sleeping, resting for the next arduous night. Dorne crossed D and continued downhill another half block. Below him huddled the Chinatown shacks, and on the next tier down were the shanties of the Paiutes who managed a precarious living hauling firewood and begging. Dorne cut through to Julia Bulette's rear door, and let himself in.

Julia was at the stove and, turning at the sound of the door, saw his battered face and choked down a cry. "Mark! Good God . . . who . . . ?"

"Sharon. In jail. I broke out, and they know it. Sorry to come here, make trouble for you with them, but Grogan. . . ."

She interrupted with a loud flutter of her full lips. "I couldn't care less about them. Sharon knows not to mess with me. Tom Peasley's boys would take all of Sun Mountain apart, and Sharon needs Tom's boys to handle his damned mine fires. Come, let me wash and doctor those filthy cuts before they become infected."

He went willingly to the laundry room. The jail floor had ground dirt into the wounds, and he did not need blood poisoning. He stripped to the waist, and Julia talked as she worked, reporting the reactions she had heard from the business community concerning the mêlée at the Opera House. There was a swell of sullen anger rising among the miners against the ring and a growing support for Adolf Sutro.

"And Grogan," she laughed. "He's mean as a rattler

today. I had to hide his clothes to keep him from rushing off to hunt for you. He's. . . ." She broke off as her day maid burst in.

"Julia, they're searching the town. The sheriff and twenty special deputies. The paper boy says they're posting big signs all over. Fifty thousand for The Major dead or alive."

Julia spun the girl about and shoved her. "Hurry, Jenny, run for Tom, tell him to come and bring troops."

The girl sped away. Dorne was already shrugging into his shirt, coat and vest over his arm, heading for the door.

Julia caught his arm and with unexpected strength hauled him back with an emphatic order. "You stay here, Mark Dorne." She jumped past him for the shotgun kept in the kitchen to discourage customers she did not want, went on to bolt the rear door, saying across her shoulder: "Shut yourself in with Grogan and stay there. They'll search the cribs, but they don't dare try that at my house. Peasley will keep them out if they try." She pointed him to the rear stairs. "I moved Grogan up there this morning with Polly to keep him occupied and out of my way. It's the front room."

Dorne went. At the corner front room he paused to knock. The sergeant had been beaten half to death, but The Major had seen him make startling recoveries before, and he did not want to surprise him in an exercise with the girl.

"It ain't locked." Shawn's gruff call was strong and welcome.

Inside, Dorne found the sergeant propped up in the bed, a small flat table across his lap, a girl in a slip facing him across it, a head-to-head poker game in progress. Grogan gaped at The Major.

"Jesus, sir, you fall in a stamp mill?"

Dorne smiled at the girl with swollen lips that slurred his

speech. " 'Morning, Polly." He then gave a short account of his capture and escape while a garble of voices grew on the street. "That will be a search party, Polly. I think Julia may need some help."

The girl slid off the bed, her mouth in a rueful twist. "Hell, Major, and just when I had a royal. Damn that crowd to hell. I hope you blast them all off the earth." She went out, her hips swaying.

Grogan saluted her with a low whistle that made her look back and flip her rump at him. Dorne tossed a gun on the bed on the way to the front window.

On D Street, an audience was gathering, watching deputies come out of houses along the row and collect in front of Julia Bulette's porch. Dorne stood behind the gauzy curtain, able to see under the porch roof from this angle.

A tall man with a wide hat was at the door, pounding on it, calling: "Sheriff, Julia. Open up."

The door slammed open, and Julia stepped out, shotgun leveled. "Get away from here, you. You don't come into my house."

The man spread his hands, placating, saying: "I'm real sorry, honey. You know I wouldn't normally, but that wild man's on the loose again, and we got orders to search every place!"

The shotgun never wavered. Julia told him hotly: "Fred, chum, don't you ever call me honey. Now, listen, you know very well that I have guests who sleep late, important men who will have your hide if you break in on them. So look somewhere else."

"Damn it, Julia, I don't want trouble with you, but I got a job to do . . . my duty."

"Your duty to Sharon? You trot on back and tell Bill

Sharon Julia Bulette says you can't come in here or so help me I'll blow your legs off."

And she might, Dorne thought, as the sheriff took a backward step, and he knew the man believed it, too. This handsome woman, queen of the camp, beloved of the fire companies, was far too popular to arrest for anything short of murder in public. The sheriff stood huffing in indecision, and the stalemate drew out. Julia, playing for time, walked at the man until he backed off the porch.

It was long enough. Yells from the side street swept through D. Tom Peasley at the head of twenty firemen came loping down the steep grade, and behind them others dragged the pumper. Peasley bulled a path through the audience with his broad shoulders, shoved past the deputies, confronting the tall sheriff, his fists balled.

"Fred Jenks, what the hell do you think you're doing?"

Jenks, red-faced with anger, shook a finger toward the porch and bawled: "Peasley, tell this damned woman to put that scatter-gun down and move out of the way. We have to search the house."

Peasley's big jaw jutted forward, and he barked: "Search it for what?"

"That murdering Major is loose . . . and in town . . . and we have to find him."

"How do you know?"

The sheriff's voice went up in furious frustration to a shrill bluster. "We had him in jail. He broke out and damned near blew up the courthouse doing it."

"Why do you think he'd come here?"

"He was seen coming this way . . . crossing C . . . he's down here somewhere."

Peasley's tone dripped contempt for Major Mark Dorne. "Probably hiding in an Indian shack. Go look through the hole down there. But you'll not put one toe inside this house."

Sheriff Fred Jenks smoked. "Peasley, you are obstructing justice. If you don't move her, I'll run you into the poke yourself."

A broad grin stretched Peasley's wide mouth. He turned, strode through the deputies to the firemen, throwing a hand signal. The men with the pumper ran forward with the hose, and the pumping team bent to the handles, riding them rhythmically up and down.

Jenks and the deputies jumped, but too late. Water sluiced from the big nozzle, drenching them all. Jenks, furious, slapped for his gun, swung it up on Peasley, and squeezed the trigger. The hammer clicked on the cartridge rim. The hard stream had driven in and drowned the powder charge.

Jenks stumbled back under the onslaught, and sat down. Deputies were flung to the ground, knocked away by the drilling force. They scrambled and charged the firemen, swinging rifle butts like scythes. Those firemen, not controlling the hose or pump, fought back with shining, bright painted axes to keep the lawmen away from the pumper.

The soaking brawl spread. The watching crowd cheered the fight, and dodged when the nozzle chased the deputies irrespective of whom it hit. One deputy did get to the pump and laid his rifle over the head of the nearest fireman as he rose on an upstroke of the handle. When he fell away, another fireman broadsided his axe at the deputy, the blade biting into the shoulder, cutting deep. There was other bloodshed, washed away in pink rivulets as the snaking stream played across the battle.

The sheriff, desperate, jumped on the porch intent on Julia Bulette. She fired between his feet with the only dry gun of anyone near. The sheriff roared, turned, and dived for safety, and the hose caught him, flung him on in a stumbling dash that took him down the slippery, muddy road, barely keeping his feet. Seeing him run, the deputies broke off and rushed after him. The search party was routed.

Tom Peasley stood, spread-legged, laughing hugely. The pumpers left off. The stream sagged to a dribble. The laughter was contagious among the firemen and the crowd alike, and a roaring cheer filled the street. Peasley waved a friendly hand at the boosters, left his boys to take in the hose and parade the pumper back to the firehouse, and went indoors with Julia.

Beside The Major at the bedroom window, Shawn Grogan guffawed. "Now, by God, that was a show to see. Hey, where you going?"

"To thank Peasley. Want me to send Polly back?"

"Hell, what I want is clothes. This is no time for games. Get me my pants."

Dorne nodded, closed the door after himself, and went down the stairs. Julia and Peasley were in the big front room, Peasley holding her while she rocked and shook with waves of laughter. The fireman threw his free arm over The Major's shoulder and beat on his back, his face glowing.

Dorne smiled in admiration. "That was magnificent, Tom. Many thanks."

"Pleasure's all mine," Peasley cawed. "Any time I can throw a monkey wrench in Sharon's gears, I'm happy to do it. Sorry about Adolf's meeting. Say, Major, I've been dreaming up some other ways you could really clobber the ring. If you could cut off the timber they need to shore up their tunnels and drifts . . . or somehow shut down the water supply for the mills . . . mills can't work ore without water."

"That's thinking big," Dorne approved. "I'll buy both ideas. But just now I need one to take Grogan out of town. Your sheriff will be back with dry powder and, I think, reinforcements from Sharon's bully boys to take this house, and it's half a day until dark. Julia, would you take your girls for an outing in your carriage as soon as they can be ready?"

Julia quit laughing, and her eyes glowed as she understood. She left, flying up the stairs to rouse the girls to a flurry of activity. Dorne was astounded by the speed with which her roomy carriage was drawn up at the rear, hitched to the four-horse matched team, the driver adjusting his gala uniform as he made ready on the high seat.

Tom Peasley and Mark Dorne hurried Shawn Grogan to the carriage, laid him on the floor of the back seat. Dorne stretched out on the front floor. The four hastily painted girls in showy costumes piled into the back, Julia and Peasley taking the front passenger seat. There were buffalo robes draped over laps, legs, and the two fugitives. In stately procession, the driver took the carriage up the grade to S Street, turned toward the pass, and walked the team between two laden ore wagons the full length of Virginia, over the crest, down toward Gold Hill.

Men on the sidewalks turned to wave at the girls, who waved back, calling greetings. Sheriff Fred Jenks, hurrying to reorganize his search party, saw them pass. Julia's outings, no novelty in the camp, were designed to display her ladies and/or to celebrate some occasion. He was too intent on his own problems to wonder how Julia had put together an outing so quickly, but it left a bitter taste that she and Tom would flaunt their recent victory in this manner.

It was a slow drive down the twisting road that narrowed to a gorge. Nowhere could they pass the ore wagons because of the heavy upcoming traffic. Dorne sweat, not from the heat under the thick fur robe, but expecting at any moment a party of riders to overtake the carriage, stop it, and discover its extra passengers.

Yet they came into Gold Hill unchallenged. There was only the single roadway, crowded on both sides by buildings that climbed the steep hillsides with no convenient side streets on which to turn off and unload the unseen passengers. There was no choice other than moving out of the stream of ore wagons and parking against the wooden sidewalk.

The driver pulled up the team. Tom Peasley waited until three following wagons had gone by, then he off-loaded the girls in a swirl of bright skirts. Dorne and Grogan slipped out in the confusion and, with a girl on each arm, followed Peasley and Julia. They paraded boldly to the corner where a flight of stairs cut out of the earth would take foot traffic to the higher houses.

"We'll be up in the brush," Dorne said. "We'll wait for the horses there . . . after it's good and dark. And, Tom, please make sure my saddlebags come. And . . . thanks to all of you."

Tom nodded. "I'll be bringing them myself, Major. Good luck."

Grogan's legs were still somewhat weak. Dorne held his arm, boosting him a bit from step to step and weaving a little himself. Anyone who might be looking saw a pair of drunks staggering up the mountain.

Chapter Eleven

Lake Tahoe, jewel of the Sierras, glistened like a vast blue carpet in its bowl under the noonday sun. At its shore, Major Mark Dorne reined in, took stock of Shawn Grogan who had healed and recovered his strength in the week of slow travel through the hills. They had ridden at night up the denuded lower slopes, and only today, sixty miles west of Virginia City and ten thousand feet above the valley floor, had Dorne felt it safe to move by daylight.

"Ready for grub?" Dorne asked.

"More than ready." The sergeant swung out of his saddle, filling his lungs with the pine-spiced air that blew from the heights across the lake. "Smells better, don't it? But that lumbering sure has played hell with the timber, even way up here."

Once there had been dense forest, before Washoe had become the mining capital of the world. Then, as the shafts went down and the miles of tunnels burrowed through Sun Mountain, millions of feet of timbering was needed to shore up the rock walls and keep the stopes from caving. The lumberjacks had come, slashing down trees hundreds of years old, stripping the east slopes higher, farther and farther up the Sierra. Nothing but stumps were left in Washoe Valley, clear around the lake, and the cutting was climbing toward the highest crest. It was now a desolate, man-scarred scene.

From the present sites, logs were tumbled down into the lake, chained within great booms, and towed across by small steamers to the east shore. Here a chute had been built down the mountainside to the desert floor and across that to Lake Washoe. Logs fed into the chute sluiced at the speed of a waterfall all the way and shot like cannon balls off the end into the lower lake. From there they were dragged out and hauled up the new grade from Washoe Valley to the mines.

Dorne and Grogan had followed the line of the chute, watching the three- to four-foot thick trunks drive by like giant toothpicks, butt to butt as a boom above was emptied. Half an hour before they reached the lake, the logs had stopped coming. Now, as Dorne looked across the water, the plume of a steamer's smoke was nearing the far shore, another moving at a snail's pace toward the chute. Grogan looked speculatively from the oncoming craft to the little, blunt nosed fishing boat, lying upside down on the bank beside the mouth of the chute.

"Think I got time, sir, to get us a couple of trout for dinner?"

"Plenty." Dorne opened his saddlebags, found a spool of line with a hook attached, and tossed it to the sergeant. "You ought to find a grub or two under a rock."

Grogan chose a dead branch left by the cutting crews, overturned the boat, tossed the oars from beneath it inside, found his bait, and shoved off along the shore. Dorne got busy getting a fire going, meanwhile silently thanking Tom Peasley for the care he'd taken to supply their horses with well-stocked saddlebags and blanket rolls. Even the last packet of dynamite sticks, which he'd taken from the cave, was tucked firmly and safely in his saddlebags. He wore the vest but not all the spaces for sticks were full.

By the time the fire was going and coffee made, the sergeant was back with two fine fish and spitted them on sticks to cook. They ate leisurely, while the loaded steamer crawled toward them.

"You figure out yet what we're going to do about this operation?" Grogan asked. "Blow up the chute?"

"Maybe later," Dorne thought aloud. "Do it now and it would tip our hand, and they could build it again too quickly. It wouldn't hurt too much. The steamers are a better target. It costs a lot of money and time to get them up here. First, though, I want to see the whole picture, find what else is vulnerable."

The steamer was not yet half across the lake when they cleaned camp, mounted, and began the long trip around the end of Lake Tahoe.

Two days later they heard the whine of saws and bite of axes, rode past a skid that dumped logs into the water, and turned uphill at the far corner of the lake. They passed teams dragging timbers to the skid, and then found the camp, a large one, with solid log walls against the cold.

At the cook house, Dorne asked for the foreman, and was directed to a small cabin set apart, and they rode to it. Dorne dismounted, tossed the reins to Grogan, rapped on the door, and pushed it in. Two men were inside, studying a map on the far wall. They turned when they heard the door.

Dorne said: "One of you the foreman?"

The taller man, heavy-set and with graying hair, waggled a hand. "Me. Peterson. What do you want?"

"Jobs for me and my partner. I'm Bud Jones. He's Shawn Kelly."

"What kind of jobs?"

"We can handle teams, any team you have."

Peterson looked interested. "You're on. Report to Belick

down at the main barn. He'll show you how to skid a log."
He turned his attention back to the map, saying over his
shoulder: "Three seventy-five a day."

The Major went back to Grogan, his smile twisted. "We
are now 'skinners for the Sierra Timber Company at three
seventy-five a day, Bill Sharon's munificence."

Grogan grunted his relief. "At least, it ain't on one end
of a saw. I had enough of that as a kid in Michigan."

They rode to the barn, dismounted outside, and tied the
horses. The building was big enough to look like stables at a
cavalry post. Inside five hostlers were cleaning stalls, a tall,
thin man overseeing the work. Dorne asked if he was Belick
and was told, no, Belick was back in the tack room at the
end of the barn. That, too, was large, with two men there,
repairing harness. A third, his hair a white halo, was in-
specting a broken tug chain, but looked up as Dorne again
introduced himself and asked for Belick. Belick's face
lighted with a wide grin.

"Praise the day, lads, we're short-handed as hell.
Where'd you learn to skid?"

"Around Michigan."

"That ought to mean you know the job, so settle in.
Fetch your saddles here, turn in your horses at the corral
out back. Stow your gear in Bunkhouse Two. Old Dilly will
assign you bunks, and, time you get that done, there'll be
chow call."

They went out to the horses, rode to the corral, and got
down to unsaddle. Sheltered from other eyes between the
animals, Dorne took off his vest, packed it in his saddlebags, and secured it. In the tack room it should not draw attention, but in the bunkhouse the crew could be expected
to pry through a new man's gear as part of the hazing that
was normal.

Bunkhouse Two was one of four, a long, log building empty except for a short one-armed man in a tiny office cluttered with brooms. Dorne guessed Dilly had had a forest accident and been pensioned as a janitor, and wondered if Sharon knew he was kept on the payroll. He doubted it. While he told the man Belick had sent them, Dilly's eyes went over them with bright inquisitiveness, then he pointed down the room.

"Clear to the back, them last two bunks, all that's empty this week. Man had the lower, a tree fell on him. Upper was a 'breed died of bad liquor."

Dorne and Grogan carried their bedrolls down the long room, the sergeant muttering that it sounded like an unhealthy corner as he threw his blanket on the top bunk. Dorne opened his on the lower, and transferred an assortment of what was in it to his pockets, stowed the rest on the floor underneath, and spread the blanket.

Outside, the loud clanging of an iron bar on a triangle signaled the end of the workday. The sound of voices grew as men and teams came out of the trees. The animals were taken to the barn, the saws and axes to the tool house, and the crews gathered in the wash shed.

Dorne and Grogan joined them at the long bench where they sloshed water from pails into tin basins, and scrubbed with raw lye soap. Many were surly with fatigue, weathered men with blackened, scarred hands and missing fingers. No one took notice of the newcomers.

After scrubbing, they cued up in the cook house with tin plates, moving past the serving crew who ladled out stewed beef, baked beans with blackstrap molasses, slabs of bread, and a quarter of a dried-apple pie piled on top. At the end of the serving counter each man picked up a quart mug of black coffee, and went on to the rows of long, oilcloth-covered tables, sitting on the benches.

There was little talking. For ten hours that day these men had muleskinned balky teams through the stumps, dragging the great logs to the skid, and now were weary and ravenous.

Across the table from Dorne and Grogan sat a man as big as either had ever seen, six feet six or more, topped with shoulder-length yellow hair straight as an Indian's, round blue eyes, and a face unmistakably Swedish. He stoked rather than ate, pushing the food onto his knife with the bread, and stabbing it into a bear trap mouth. He cleaned a heaped plate twice and put down three slabs of pie, never raising his head but his eyes, under the light brows, going back and forth between Grogan and Dorne. When there was no more food before him, he sat back, his heavy jaw shoved out, and picked at his square teeth with the knife point.

"Who the hell are you?" He spoke around the knife belligerently.

Dorne gave him the new names. "We've just hired on."

The blond giant touched his chest with the blade. "Ole Swensen. I'm king of the mountain. Don't forget it."

"Interesting." Dorne's tone was flat, unimpressed. He knew the term that came out of the Michigan woods, a title claimed by a bully as long as he could beat any challengers in the brutal fights of the timber camps. Finished with his supper, he got up, turned his back, and walked out with Grogan.

At this altitude the evening air was twenty degrees cooler than in Virginia City.

Grogan buttoned his coat, saying: "Did you ever see hands that big, sir? That guy could maul a grizzly."

Dorne knew it was not fear in the awed voice. In the regiment the sergeant had been noted for settling arguments not by rank but with his fists, and, if the Swede had this impact on Grogan, it meant the man was truly dangerous. He smiled. "We'll soon see what he can do. You cold?"

"A little," Grogan admitted. "I'm not all back in shape, I guess."

They headed for the bunkhouse, noisy now with the men fed and somewhat rested. Three card games were starting at the tables between the bunks, and someone was mourning on a harmonica. Heads turned to watch them go down the room, then a quick silence fell. Into that a voice behind Dorne carried to the corners.

"You got my whisky, tenderfoot?"

Dorne turned without hurry, tilting his head back to look at the huge Swede. "Your whisky, Swensen?"

The wide mouth spread in a hungry grin. "Didn't you hear? New men have to get me a bottle from the company store every week the first month they're here or go down the hill with a busted head. Chase yourself over before they lock up."

Major Mark Dorne's fist was lightning fast. The greatest military tactic was surprise. This man had better than a four inch reach on him and outweighed him a hundred pounds, but he was full of food, and, if he was slow, he was vulnerable. Dorne's fist went deep in a roll of fat put on by too much booze and too many slabs of pie. The big man almost doubled over. Dorne followed with a knee hard into the groin. As the head came farther down, he drove his fist under the heavy jaw. The head snapped back. The king of the mountain reeled.

Like driving pistons, Dorne followed with a right and a left against the jaw without effect, then two more to the stomach. A sharp belch erupted. He might as well be hitting a granite block.

The giant's arms looped around him, crushing. Unless The Major broke that grip, he would be squeezed in half, and there was only one way to prevent it. Dorne threw himself in a backward arc, took the Swede off balance to fall on top of him. He flung out his arms to break the fall, but it knocked out his breath.

For an instant The Major lay, filling his empty lungs, then heaved the bewildered bully aside, and rolled out from under. He was on his feet before the other could raise to his knees and aimed a kick at the man's head. His boot toe caught the temple. Swensen collapsed on his face, not moving. Dorne waited to be sure, then looked at the dazed faces, watching.

"Anyone else?" His voice was somewhat breathless but strong.

There was no answer. The men might not even have heard. All attention was on the still figure on the floor. Dorne turned his back and walked to his bunk where Grogan sat with a drawn gun. The Major raised one eyebrow at the gun. Grogan looked sheepish.

"I wasn't sure you could take him, and I thought I'd better be ready if his friends wanted to play, too."

Dorne smiled. "Put it away, Shawn. A king of the mountain doesn't have any real friends, any more than a king of a country. It's lonely up there."

Grogan started to holster the gun, then stopped, looking beyond Dorne and saying sharply: "Behind you, sir."

The Major spun, on balance. The big Swede moved, crawled to his feet, stood turning on unsteady legs as though he were disoriented. Then he lumbered at a jolting gait to the door, and shoved through it. In the silent room, they could hear the well pump screech, needing grease, and, before the lumberjacks came out of their trance, the big

107

man staggered back. His head dripping, he went directly to Dorne and stopped in front of him.

He stood half crouched, maintaining his balance as his eyes ranged up and down the smaller man with wonder. Then he put his right hand forward tentatively. Grogan thought it was the opening move of a new round, a positioning for a wrestle. He lifted the gun. Swensen did not even see it. The slash mouth spread to a grin that crowded his cheeks against his ears.

"You one helluva whirlwind, man. Py God, Ole Swensen know he meet a buzz saw. Tomorrow I bring *you* the whisky."

Mark Dorne accepted the hand gingerly. His own could be crushed by that great paw. Swensen engulfed it as gently as he would handle a raw egg. Then he wavered back up the room, and collapsed on his bunk.

Chapter Twelve

From that night, the giant Swede dogged Mark Dorne's steps, a watchdog to protect a new master from any further initiation harassment. By extension, Shawn Grogan was included in the protection to the sergeant's embarrassment.

For a month they skidded logs. Dorne accumulated information about the lumbering operation, looked for weak spots, acquainted himself with the crews, learned their temper. Rough men they were, simple men, brawling, laughing, singing, drinking, and dancing wild heavy steps through the Saturday nights. Their three seventy-five was good pay to them as against the miners' three fifty. They looked down on the men who spent their lives in the black bowels of the earth, felt themselves lords on the towering slopes in the free, clean air. Defiant individualists, Dorne saw indications that they would draw together in a tight clan against an outside threat. He believed, if he could create such an impression, he could use Ole Swensen as a leader they would rally to. Meanwhile, both Dorne and Grogan let their hair, mustaches, and beards grow. There was little resemblance now to the posters of The Major.

For that month, there'd been no raids against the ring's properties. Bill Sharon did not know whether to rejoice or worry. The calm was a sword over his head. He hoped The Major was dead, and the troubles over. But he could not be sure. It made him nervous. At last he made a trip to San Francisco to confer with Ralston.

He paced the ornate office of the Bank of California, his

mouth pursed, brow furrowed, jumpy.

"Where is he? What's he doing if he's alive? I feel like he's breathing over my shoulder. Breathing fire. All I'm sure of is that he's not in Virginia City, and he hasn't been seen since the day he blew the jail. Julia Bulette and Tom Peasley drove our search party off, and then went riding. We thought it was to decoy my boys away from the house, and we went in while they were gone. No Major, no Grogan there. Bill, we combed that town end to end and had a circle around it to watch for him. We looked in the firehouse to see if Peasley had them hidden. No. They vanished like smoke."

"Calm down." Ralston sat, big and powerful, smiling easily. "They are probably both dead. With the price on his head, somebody would have turned The Major up by now, and the Army's hunting Grogan. But if they are alive, there's a way to smoke them out. The man is after money. He succeeded in taking one shipment. It appears to me the raids were a prelude to an attempt to blackmail us for more."

"It's not just that. It's vengeance. His father was killed when we broke the strike at Calico. His mother went mad. He went on the warpath to pay us back."

"Oh?" Ralston's brows went up. "How do you know?"

"You don't?" Sharon was surprised, then snapped his fingers. "But, of course, you were in Europe at the time."

He took a wallet from his breast pocket, fished from it a clipping of the scathing editorial Arthur McEwan had run in the *Enterprise* naming himself and Mark Dorne as two men who would not bow to arrogant power and its misuse, and passed it to Ralston.

The banker read it, let it drop on the desk, saying with sudden anger: "Why wasn't I told about this?"

"At the time, the article didn't seem important. By the time you returned, I suppose I took it for granted you had seen it."

Sharon saw the anger rise in the other man. He knew that busy as Ralston was, with his fingers in a hundred projects, the man insisted on knowing, in detail, of any danger that threatened his beloved bank and knew his explanation wasn't satisfactory. He wanted to explain further but knew better. He waited, seeing Ralston force his anger down in order to concentrate on solutions, drumming his fingers impatiently on the desk, brow furrowed.

Finally Ralston said: "Money is still the key, though. He needs it to fight us. Let us use it as bait to learn if he is still able to fight. Sharon, we have always been secretive in shipping gold coin for the mine payrolls and local Washoe expenses. This time we will let the newspapers hear we are sending five million to cover the next six months. That should bring him running if he isn't in his grave."

Sharon was horrified. "An actual shipment?"

"Certainly."

"Good God, with everybody knowing it, how could we protect it?"

Ralston smiled again, the smile of a hunter sure of his game. "By taking a leaf from The Major's own book. He uses dynamite. We ship in iron chests. They will be loaded at the mint and hauled by Wells Fargo to the express office of the new railroad, put aboard a sealed freight car, and that hooked on the end of the regular transcontinental train. Somewhere between Sacramento and Reno that car will be shunted onto a siding and replaced with another containing identical chests . . . weighted, of course, and rigged with powder and fuse . . . to blow when the chests are opened. With the first lift of a lid, The Major is blown to hell where he belongs."

Sharon slowly sat down, holding onto the chair arms with both hands, his voice weak at the prospect. "You . . . think the papers . . . would feature a routine movement?"

"Hardly routine." Ralston's voice was dry. "This will be the first time we have shipped the payrolls by rail. The railroad promoters will make the most of it. It will be page one news without doubt."

"But . . . if he's some place where he doesn't see a paper?"

"We'll see the story is run far enough in advance that he gets wind of it."

It was Shawn Grogan who saw the story in the *Nevada Times*. One of a newly recruited crew brought the issue to the lumber camp, and it passed from hand to hand to men starved for news of the outside. Grogan lay in his bunk reading while Mark Dorne played a listless game of nickel and dime poker to pass the evening. The sergeant sat up abruptly, signaled Dorne. After a few minutes, Dorne cashed in, wandered idly to the bunk. Grogan handed him the paper with the black block type across the head.

"Five . . . million dollars, gold, sir. Sounds mighty tempting."

"Too tempting." The Major dropped the paper, smiling. "It sounds phony. Why would they publicize a shipment of that size this time? They never have before."

Disappointed at the reaction, Grogan argued: "The article says they never shipped by rail before. Why couldn't it be the railroad that wants to show how important it is?"

"I'm sure it's that, too, and we'll look into it . . . later. Before we leave here, though, I want to send the ring another message."

"You decided what and how yet?"

Another of the lumberjacks came by, asked if Grogan was finished with the newspaper. The sergeant gave it to him, and the man sat down on the next bunk. Dorne tipped his head toward the door and strolled outside with Grogan where they would not be overheard. They walked as far as the skid to be sure no one was in the shadows around the buildings and stood looking down on the inky lake.

Dorne said: "The steamers, Shawn. Those two boats are the weakest link up here. It takes six months to build them. If they're destroyed, this operation shuts down while they're replaced."

Grogan's growl was deep in his throat. "Blow them up, sir?"

"Not the first one. You don't know enough about dynamite for us to blow both at the same time, and blasting one would be a warning to look to the other. There's another fishing boat the boys use on this side. I'll borrow that, follow the night steamer well out, and open the sea cocks. Sink her."

"Major," the sergeant sounded eager. "I got my own score to settle with those birds. Let me do this job, will you?"

"All right. You earned it. We'll tie onto the boom, ride it to the deepest part of the lake. I'll put you aboard there and pick you up when she goes down."

"The crew . . . they didn't do anything to us. How do they get to shore?"

"The steamer carries a lifeboat and life rings. And if they can't launch it in time, they can hang onto logs . . . logs don't sink. They'll be picked up when it's daybreak."

"Sounds good, Major. Do we go tonight?"

"The moon won't be full until tomorrow night, but we'll go down and show you the valves."

The steamer was tied against the dock, dark and empty, the crew ashore because there were no bunks on the small vessel. By starlight Dorne found the companionway to the engine room, dropped into it, and lit the lantern there for Grogan. When the sergeant came down, The Major opened the panel that led to the bilges and there pointed out the row of valves, saying: "With all those open, she'll sink in minutes. Don't worry about the fireman being here. When they're under way, he goes on deck, out of the heat until the boilers need stoking again."

Back in the engine room, Dorne turned out the lantern, hung it where he had found it, trailed Grogan up to the rail, and over it to the dock. Out of the darkness a voice surprised them.

"What you doing on the boat, chums?"

There was no mistaking Ole Swensen's inflections. Dorne thought he might have expected the Swede to show up. Every time he looked around the giant was nearby. This time it made a problem. One company rule barred everyone except the crews from the steamers. He might get a promise from the big man not to mention seeing them here, but there was no guarantee he might not let it slip. He would have to meet this head on and afterward judge what to do.

"Ole," he said earnestly, "I could tell you we were just curious, but that wouldn't be true, and I won't lie to you. Listen to what I'll tell you. I'm trusting my life . . . both our lives . . . to you in doing it." He could not see Swensen's face clearly, would have to tell by the breathing what reaction there would be. He described what he found when he first got to Washoe, his dead and bloodied father, his mindless mother, the vicious attack on the strikers. He told of the vow he had made, and what he had done to keep it.

Swensen's breath went in and out with long, hissing sounds and muttered curses.

"Tomorrow night, Ole, Grogan and I mean to sink this steamer. The next night, when the other sails, we'll sink that. With them gone, the delivery of logs will stop for six months. Without shoring timber and firewood for the boilers, the mines will be crippled for that long. It will cost the ring millions. What will you do about it?"

There was not a moment's hesitation in the answer. "What I do, py God, I help you."

The Major did not need the help, but if Swensen was involved, it was fair insurance he would watch his tongue. Gravely he accepted the offered hand.

Chapter Thirteen

All afternoon thunderheads built mountains of clouds above the solid peaks, and wind lashed the lake to running whitecaps. A boom could not be hauled across in those stormy waters. The free-floating logs inside would be thrown over the chained ones containing them. Dorne put off the idea of a sinking that night. Yet, after dark, the wind dropped to calm, and rain began. The foreman decided on sending the steamer to keep on schedule.

Dorne took Grogan and Swensen to the shore where the fishing boat was pulled into the tule reeds. Grogan had the bow seat, Dorne the stern, and Swensen claimed the oars, his massive physical strength of most use there. They waited until the steamer left the dock, picked up the boom in tow, and headed outbound into the dark. No one stayed on shore in the drenching downpour to watch after it. Still, Dorne kept them where they were until the steamer was a quarter mile off. Then they went after it. Swensen's strong strokes soon overhauled the boom, and they tied to that for a free ride to the center depths.

At the head of the long boom they could not see the steamer. Lights aboard would blind the skipper. The only one used was a headlamp beamed off the bow to locate loose logs the afternoon wind might have floated into their course. They had glimpses of the pale beam through the rain curtain as it was swept from side to side. The black sky hung low, and they rode through a world of water.

Dorne had timed the trips day after day. When the steamer was near the center of the lake, he gave his order.

"Cast off, Shawn. Ole, take us up where Shawn can board her."

The big Swede bent to the oars. The little craft surged alongside the boom and pulled against the steamer. No one was on the drenched deck to see them. Swensen stood up, took Grogan on his shoulders, and raised him high enough to reach the rail. From there the sergeant pulled himself up and over. Swensen then took the boat off into the dark where they would not be spotted if someone did come out of the cabin. Staying out of the arc of the headlamp, they stood by to take Grogan off when he would signal he was ready.

On board, Shawn Grogan moved along the solid cabin wall to the companionway. The door faced the stern and was closed. Light leaked around the edges. Grogan put his ear against it and listened and, when he heard no sound, reached for the handle. But heavy steps came down the deck, and he ducked around the corner. A man turned the other corner, opened the door, and clattered down the steps. Grogan heard the door of the firebox *clang* open, then a chunk of wood thrown in on the burning pile. Shortly the man came up again and went away. It had been close, but Grogan was pleased that he would not have to hurry.

He slipped inside and was further pleased to find a whisky bottle half full on the floor beneath the hanging lantern, told himself it would be a waste to let it go to the bottom, and enjoyed a long pull before he took the lantern into the bilge.

To use both hands he set the lantern on the walkway and began turning valves. The water came fast. As he opened the last sea cock, it rose over his shoes, hissed against the glass lantern chimney, broke that, and doused the flame. It did not matter. He could feel his way back.

He was close to the engine room door when someone there cursed: "What put that damn lantern out? Can't see my bottle."

Grogan froze. The fireman must have forgotten to take the whisky with him and had come back for it. He was embarrassed at his own failure to realize this. He had to move or be trapped, with the water now sloshing above his ankles. The fireman struck a match, peering around for the lantern that was not there. The match burned down to his fingers, and he dropped it. If the sergeant stayed where he was, he could drown in the dark bilge.

Grogan tried a dash past the man, but the other had just struck another match, saw him, yelled, and dropped the second match. Grogan, in mid-charge across the engine room, ran into the fireman and drove him stumbling against the firebox. The hot metal wrenched another cry from the man and reflex bounded him off. A swinging fist he could not see cracked hard against Grogan's face, rocked the sergeant back on his heels. The fireman came on, groping through the dark, connected with Grogan's shoulder, giving Grogan a target. He sent over a looping left that slammed against bone thinly covered with flesh.

The sergeant took a blow under the heart in return, staggered, and gave ground. In the black space he could not make out the direction of the companionway. Turning, trying to feel a draft or see a lighter rectangle of sky, he stepped in a spot of oil, slipped, and went down to one knee. Then the fireman was on him again, flailing roundhouse blows on the chance of hitting something solid. Grogan sensed the arms sweeping over his head, then the man's knees struck his shoulder, and he stumbled. Instinctively Grogan wrapped his arms around the legs. The man came down in a heavy fall.

They lay tangled, gasping. Grogan felt smothered by the hot air, but he was first to recover. He rolled free, against a wall, dragged himself up it, fumbled along it until it ended at the companionway, and scrambled up the steps.

On deck the cool night air and slashing rain cleared his head. He expected attack up there, but there was none. The muffled noise of the fight below had not carried to the cabin. He jumped for the rail, feeling along it, trying to see through the rain that streamed over his eyes, to locate the little boat standing by. His hand touched a life ring. He fumbled to unfasten it from the rail. If he could free it, he could jump, swim away from the steamer, and call to The Major.

There was not time. The fireman burst up the companionway shouting. Now the cabin heard, and feet erupted, slapping toward him on the deck. A lantern was lit inside and brought out, held high to illuminate as much as possible. Rain refracted the glow, kept it to a small ball of light. It did not reach Grogan but did show him dark shapes running at him.

The sergeant drew his gun. He had deserved his sharpshooter medal in the 7th Cavalry. His shot exploded the lantern. Flaming oil showered down on the man who held it. He screamed as it spilled down his face. He dropped the handle and buried his face in his hands. Points of light winked as his dry clothes caught. Dark silhouettes crowded around him to strip off the flaming clothes and fling them to the deck.

The steamer was built of local pine loaded with resin. The planks were drenched, but the resin blazed up in running rivulets along the seams of pitch. Fire ate into the boards themselves. A whirling holocaust of flame spread rapidly over the deck, turned the rain curtain glittering red, and against that black figures ran toward the lifeboat hanging amidships.

Shawn Grogan still could not see Dorne's craft. The hurricane of fire was leaping toward him. He stayed no longer, flung himself over the rail, and dropped into the fire-lit lake. It was icy, snow water run-off from the higher crests that closed over him as he sank. It chilled him through. He was numb by the time he broke the surface, coming up.

He began swimming away from the burning ship, hoping Mark Dorne would see him against the red backdrop. The heavy boots dragged at his feet, his thick clothes encumbered his arms, and the cold sapped his strength. His clumsy strokes were not enough to buoy him. He gasped in air, but sank.

For the first time in his life Shawn Grogan knew cold fear. He had faced Confederate charges, stood firm when howling Indians raced their ponies at him, confident in his and his troop's abilities. But alone in this icy black depth was another matter. He rallied, kicked upward, pumped his arms, broke the surface again, dragged in air but knew he could not stay on top. His arms were leaden. There was no feeling in his legs. He could not tell if he was still using them. Tiredness filled his cold, numbed body. It lulled him, washed away the terror. What difference did it make? Why should he go on struggling? The deep water pulled at him, drew his head down. He stopped moving, sucked in, filled his lungs with water, felt at peace.

He was being dragged against wood, mauled, tumbled, jarred on his stomach, his back crushed, half conscious. He felt a hot flood from his mouth, and lay enduring, too weak to protest. It seemed the torture continued for hours while the hot flood pulsed. Between the crushings, he gagged. At last his body rebelled, fought back, his lungs sucked again, filled with air.

The pressure on his back stopped. Strong hands lifted his shoulders, turned him over, eased him to a sit with his legs stretched before him. Groggy, he opened his eyes. He was on the bottom of the boat, Mark Dorne crouched before him in a red suit, red-faced, red-eyed, slapping his face. He turned his head aside.

Behind him Ole Swensen's voice was gruff. "The big fish wakes up now. Good."

Dorne heaved a sigh, and smiled. "Sorry we couldn't get here quicker. I almost didn't find you."

Grogan coughed, and the last of the water rushed out. He wiped his mouth with the back of a hand and said in wonder: "Know something, sir? First time I ever gave up, but it felt so comfortable." The sergeant discovered the hair plastered against Dorne's head and the puddle he crouched in. "You went in after me?"

"You were ten feet down. I'd have missed you if I hadn't kicked you. Now look at your steamer."

It was a thousand feet away, an island of fire in a hissing red lake, all but obscured in smoke. The rain had slacked to drizzle, and through that and the smoke flames reached like lightning for the sky.

"The crew," Grogan said, "do you know if they all got off?"

"Yes, six men. Two were cut off from the lifeboat, but they used the rings. They're hanging to the boom. What started the fire?"

Grogan explained. "But I didn't expect the boat to catch, wet as it was."

"Good that it did. When you were seen, they could have closed the sea cocks and saved her."

The hissing rose to a gale sound, the steamer settling deeper, the engine weight at the stern pulling it down, pulling the end of the boom with it. Logs floated out of the confine. But the buoyancy of the many logs was too much for the linkage between them. It snapped. Those chained, great trunks that had gone under, shot to the surface, and on into the air, fell back, and drifted free.

The light was gone. There were cries in the dark. The lifeboat party located the two on the rings. There was a clamor as they were pulled aboard. Then the lake was silent.

The Major asked Grogan: "Did anyone on board get a good look at you? Were you recognized?"

"The fireman saw me plain. I guess he could describe me. So could the men on deck."

"Then we'll have to pull out. There'll be a hunt for whoever sank the boat . . . and then they'll know we're missing."

The sergeant groaned. "And leave the other one afloat? Can't we get rid of her first?"

"Too much risk now. They'll guard her well. Ole, row while I lay out a plan. Head around the long point so we aren't seen from the dock. When we land, before the lifeboat gets in to report, Grogan can catch up our horses while I get the duffel from the bunkroom. Meet me at the barn for the saddles."

Swensen, digging in the oars, said: "I'm going with you. I cut no more timber for Sharon."

"Go help Grogan with the horses then, and I'll bring your gear."

It was a long row to shore. Ole Swensen pulled a steady rhythm. As they passed the point, the noise that carried across the water from the dock sounded as if every man in camp had run down to watch the fire. With luck they would stay there until Dorne's party had ridden out. The boat nosed into the tules. Dorne stepped into the shallow water, watched Grogan get on his feet, and took his arm to steady him. The sergeant was shaking with cold, not at all in good shape. The Major changed his orders.

"Shawn, you go straight to the barn, bring out the saddles and gear from the tack room. Ole, you get what we have from the bunkhouse. I'll catch the horses."

The rain came heavier again as they climbed the rise to the camp. It was deserted. Dorne walked with Grogan to the barn, took a coil of rope, and strode to the corral.

Thunder cracked overhead. As he reached the pole corral, a long slash of lightning showed him the enclosure, one horse against the fence, with drooping head and tail tucked under. He moved in slowly, not to frighten it, and dropped the noose over the head. It was too well trained to fight and followed him as he led it through the gate, stopped as he tied it.

He went in after another. The animals were uneasy, moving together while the lightning continued. He chose the one in the lead and cast while the sky was alight, felt the rope tighten and yank. The animal reared, fighting the rope. Dorne worked toward it hand over hand up the braided buckskin, stroked the neck until the horse stood trembling, then took it out beside the other. Like the first, the third horse gave no trouble. He was closing the gate when a voice roared close by.

"What's going on here?"

With the lead rope in his left hand, Dorne flicked out his gun, spinning in the direction of the voice. More lightning showed him a figure three feet away. With one step he was in range, raked the barrel across the head, and the man dropped. The Major stood listening, but no more sound came. The man had been alone. Dorne hurried the three horses to the barn.

Grogan and Swensen were standing with the saddles and bunkhouse gear in the dry runway, a lantern turned low. They saddled fast, were almost ready to mount when loud voices approached up the hillside. A bobbing lantern sent a yellow glow ahead.

Dorne stooped to douse the light in the barn, saying urgently: "Up, both of you, clear out of here. Meet me where the lake trail forks at the base of the point."

Grogan hesitated. Swensen caught his arm, hoisted him to make him mount, then was up himself, slapping the rump of the sergeant's horse. They drove into the night.

The party from the dock saw them and with a high yell ran to cut them off.

Chapter Fourteen

The Major judged the distances. The lumbermen, routed out of their bunks when the steamer fire was discovered, were only half-dressed and unarmed. He took time to dig out a single stick of dynamite, clamp it between his teeth before he mounted, and put the horse out of the barn where the crew could see him. They changed direction, running toward him as he intended, distracted from chasing after Grogan and Swensen.

He sat quietly in the doorway, lit the fuse, held it until it burned within an inch of exploding, then tossed it. It went off in the air short of the running men. His war was not with them. They stopped short, then fled.

Dorne rode after the sergeant and Swensen, found them at the rendezvous, and they began the long ride around the big lake. The storm worsened. Lightning and thunder became a continuous flash and roll. They kept going some ten miles before they found a cutbank cave that broke the blast of wind, and they pulled into that lee.

Swensen brought in wet branches. Dorne used fuse powder to tease a fire to life, caught a coffee pot full of water from the run-off sluicing down from the top of the cave entrance, set it to boil, then wrapped Grogan in his damp blanket. The sergeant shivered so that his coffee spilled when he held the cup for Dorne to lace it from his whisky flask.

"Get some sleep, both of you," he told them. "In the morning, you two go down to the valley. Grogan, you'll take Ole to the cave and wait for me there."

"What about you?"

"I'll be along later. First I'm going to knock out the other steamer."

The sergeant tried to straighten. "We'd better be with you to help."

His face was gray even in the firelight, drawn and sunken. It took both hands to keep the cup upright. The near drowning had set him far back from his recovery from the beating.

"You had better do as I say." It was a command. "You've helped enough for a while."

Shawn Grogan fell asleep sitting up. Dorne eased him to the ground, added his own blanket as cover. He saw Swensen sag back. He stretched out with his head on his saddlebags, dozing between trips for wood to hold the fire.

By morning the storm had passed, their clothes almost dried by the heat of the blaze. They cleaned their guns, chewed on jerked meat, drank coffee, then saddled and took up the trail toward the eastern side of the lake. Where their paths parted, Grogan resumed his argument for going with Dorne but was cut short.

"I need to travel light. The things I don't need, I've taken out of my saddlebags and divided them into each of yours, including half of my late, generous wages."

Ole interrupted, grinning. "Ole has all his last wages plus most of Belick's."

"You've been winning at cards with Belick?"

Swenson nodded, his grin widening. "Belick thinks Ole is a dummy. He thinks he read my face when I get cards. I let him think."

"And that worked?"

"Enough."

Even in his weakened condition Grogan joined in

Dorne's laughter, and the big Swede glowed.

"OK, then. You'll need some supplies. Be careful where you buy them. Shawn, you're no good to me in the shape you're in. I want you well, to help take that five million from the train. Ole, see that he rests and knock him out if he doesn't."

Ole nodded in agreement. "Then I sit on him to keep him down."

Grogan still grumbled as they turned downhill. Dorne watched them out of sight, then rode along the shore toward the chute where the steamer would deliver the next logs.

It took a day and a half before he heard voices through the screen of brushwood spared by the lumbering locusts. He tied the horse and went forward until he could see.

Apparently the scattered boom had been recovered and brought in. A crew was working on the wooden bulkhead with peavey poles and cant hooks, starting logs end on into the mouth of the chute. Lake water sluicing into it pulled them with it. They moved sluggishly, maneuvered into position by the men above, then pitched down as the sharp angle of the flume fell away, following the contour of the mountain, and disappeared at express train speed.

Another crew manned the logs in the boom with cleated boots. Standing astride, balancing against the roll, a man poled forward until his log just entered the sluice, then jumped to the water level platform, ran across the floating, moving mass for another trunk. It was dangerous, expert work. Dorne watched in admiration the sure-footed agility of the men. Then he looked across the lake. A wisp of white smoke rose against the green far shore. The steamer was heading out with another gather.

It was ten o'clock. The haul took three hours. It would not arrive until nearly one. A shout from the loggers drew his attention back there. A log had escaped the boom and was floating away. One of the crew, a redhead Dorne recognized, went for the little one-man fishing pram Grogan had used, shoved off, and rowed after the log, prodding it back with an oar as a cowboy would haze a straying steer until a cant hook man caught it. Then the redhead dragged the boat up the bank beside the chute, leaving it right side up for the next need of it.

The Major retreated to his horse, rode two miles back the way he had come, got down, and built a small fire. The wind was blowing from the direction of the work and would carry the smoke smell away from the men. He removed the vest from his saddlebags and hung it on a bush, so that any dampness left in it would be well dried and aired out. He made coffee, chewed jerked meat, and rested. When the sun had passed its zenith, Dorne shrugged into his loaded vest, and returned to the brush near the sluice.

The boom was empty. The men were hurrying now to unlink the chains and shoot those logs on their way. The little steamer was only a quarter of a mile out. Mark Dorne watched as it towed its load within two hundred yards of shore, cast off, steamed to the rear, and with its blunt prow pushed the timber against the bulkhead. The new boom was tied, then the steamer steered against a short dock parallel to the shore on the far side of the logs from Dorne, and moored to it. The boiler was shut down, the crew climbed off, bringing dinner pails for the other crew as well as for themselves. Everyone retreated down the shore to eat where they could hear themselves talk, away from the roar of the chute.

Mark Dorne thanked his luck. His main concern had

been how to empty the steamer of innocent men, and they had solved that problem for him. All he needed to do now was run the logs to where the boom floated against the steamer side, plant his charge, get back to his horse, and ride out.

But he could not run logs in riding boots. So he took them off, unbuckled his belt, ran it through the loops at their top, and fastened the belt again. He pushed them around to a position just behind his left hip. It was clumsy but practical. He automatically left his holster side free even though there was no holster, no gun. Those were back with his saddlebags, his horse. He slipped through the brush as far as it extended, then sprinted across the open space to the logs sluggishly rising and falling on the waves, blown against the shore. The great trunks were almost steady under his weight, bobbing only a little when he jumped from one to another, rolling slowly as he left them.

At the offshore side of the steamer, he boarded her. Her stern was closest to him, the companionway only steps away. As his head rose above the deck level, he could see the crews, cross-legged on the ground, eating, talking, laughing. None was looking his way. He got a hand on the rail and vaulted over, lay on his belly, wriggled to the companionway door, and went down it, head first. In the shaded room he bound three sticks of dynamite together with enough fuse to burn until he was safely on shore, placed the package not so close to either boiler or firebox that the heat would set it off too soon, and lit the fuse.

Down in that close, thick-walled space and busy with his work, he did not hear his horse whinny as it shied clear at the warning whir of a timber rattler.

By the time he had his charge settled and burning to his satisfaction and had reached the deck again, he saw men running. Three were on the dock coming up the plank they used for boarding. Dorne had no choice. He leapt forward toward the boarding plank and skidded to a stop looking into the face of the man in the lead. He wore a captain's jacket.

The man gaped, then yelled: "Here he is . . . friend of the one who sunk the Daisy. What are you . . . ?"

"Blowing this tub," Dorne shouted it. "Run!"

The captain did not run. He pulled a gun. Dorne couldn't get past the three oncoming men without a fight, and the fuse was sputtering. There was no time.

He ducked and lunged and hit the captain's gun hand, throwing the man off balance. The shot went wild. The Major turned, took the rail in a leap onto a log. The force of his landing sunk the end and spun the trunk. If he fell through the giant mass of logs, he would be crushed between them and carried by the drag of current into the chute. He fought to a precarious balance, shouting his warning of the dynamite charge. The captain fired again but missed. Dorne continued shouting as he raced the length of a log, dancing to another as it rolled.

Now the captain and the men took heed, ran down the plank, and off the dock. Two of them caught up peaveys and cant hooks, and chased Dorne. With their spiked boots they came fast and, ironically, saved him. They were too close for the captain to risk firing again.

Dorne was in the middle of a log four feet in diameter when the man with the peavey jabbed it with the sharp point, locked the hook deep, and spun it. Dorne danced to the next, felt it bob, then bob again, looked back in time to see the long cant hook swinging at his head. He dodged that, turned to meet the charge, and, when the hook came at him again, caught it, yanked, and the man sprawled on the log. It tried to roll. Dorne steadied it. The peavey man grabbed the other's shoulder just before he would have slipped off.

Dorne yelled: "Get him up, fast. You have about two minutes before she blows!"

They all ran, those behind Dorne no longer swinging at him, only hurrying to get to solid ground. Dorne reached it first. The others were steps behind when the steamer exploded. It flew apart. Débris was thrown high and wide. Concussion hit the loggers like a wall, throwing them flat. Logs near the steamer rose, end on, into the air, and plummeted back. Their shock wave rushed toward the shore, tossing the timbers into and onto each other in a thunder of crunching, grinding, thumping sound. The two men behind Dorne had not quite reached solid footing and were thrown, falling between two rolling trunks, screaming as the trunks jammed together. Dorne went back, pulled one of them free, and recognized this one as the redhead whose footwork he'd been admiring earlier. Between them they got the other man free of the jam. He helped them to shore, then ran for his horse.

Now three other loggers rushed out of the brush from that direction. They carried rifles. All that kept him alive in that moment was their shock at what they saw. They stood frozen.

Mark Dorne pivoted. There was no shelter. He ran through the open to the little punt on the bank, shoved it into the churning water between the boom and the sluice, jumped into it as it swung through the mouth of the chute. The high sides, channeled out of the ground and lined with logs, gave protection then. The men running toward him could not see him.

The current tugged the boat on. The Major helped,

prodding an oar against the side. The craft picked up speed as a man's head appeared above, blurred, as Dorne sped by. Then the chute tilted sharply down and the water boiled. Dorne sat flat in the bottom at the stern, hoping the bow would not dip and somersault. Like a nutshell, the little craft danced from side to side, buffeted by long ridges of water, and dropped into narrow valleys between them. He had no control. Even had there been a tiller, it could not have guided the bouncing boat through that falling torrent. Time and again the lighter bow and the heavier stern tried to swing the craft athwart the channel. Fortunately there was not enough width for the little craft to turn sidewise.

Dorne's sensation was of flying, of being shot from a cannon. At least there were no logs shooting down on top of him. The men above might well have peavied some in by now, but with such a head start, he thought, they could not overtake him. What could be ahead was a jam, a pile up of trunks tossed high enough to hang against the flume top where others would dash into them and dam the flow.

There were long curves around which he could not see. Beyond any of them he could be hurled into such a jam and smashed. He could not really see anything clearly. The log walls flashed by too fast, giving the impression that they were closing in on him.

The pitch continued, steep all the way down the long mountainside, then leveled somewhat for the last flat miles to Washoe Lake. But the speed did not decrease. The drive from behind was too great. Then half a mile ahead he saw a blue surface that appeared to be a wall with distant mountains on top of it. Reason told him it was the lower lake. Now another fear arose: that there would be logs floating there for him to crash into.

He could see none, no dark lengths against the blue. The

walls were too high to look over; his only view was straight ahead, a narrow gap. The walls rushed past, and then were gone. The little boat rode a jet of water, launched out over nothing, twenty feet above the lake's surface, then dropped into a churning pool without shores. The boat bobbed, swung wildly, spun around, was sluiced on through eddies until, far from the chute, it slowed and lay in calm.

Major Mark Dorne was curled on the bottom between the seats, his body shaking, his eyes closed while the rushing after view continued in his mind's eye. It was minutes before that stopped and he could steady himself and open his eyes. That was not a ride he would ever want to take twice.

When he could sit up, he was drifting in the middle of the lake. On the eastern shore, the sawmill's smoke rose in a thick plume. Saws whined, slicing timber into thick slabs for shoring. To wreck that might be another project, but not one for today. He sat huddled on the stern seat, grateful for warm sunlight.

Slowly his thoughts came together. He removed the wet, battered boots from his belt and managed to get them on. He still wore the vest, only because he needed it buttoned when he reached for a dynamite stick. The sticks that were left were sodden. He removed them and tossed them overboard. He could make more of those. The vest would be harder to replace.

He smiled wryly, conjuring up a picture of his present appearance. There was one thing good about it. This bedraggled, long-haired, bearded person certainly didn't risk being recognized for the long wanted Major Dorne—at least not until the news from the Tahoe camp had time to reach the mines and Virginia City.

On the west side of the valley under the Sierras at the

edge of the lake squatted the mansion Sandy Bowers, first millionaire of Virginia City, had built for his wife, Eilley Orrum. From this distance it looked a square box in a grove of pale green trees. In front of it ran a dust ribbon, the road to the newly named town of Reno.

Dorne slid oars out from under the seat, and only after he was rowing toward the Bowers place did he register amazement that they had still been in the craft. He didn't remember feeling them under him in the wild ride down the chute.

It took little more than a half hour to reach the beach a short distance from the mansion. He deliberately set the little craft adrift. Better that he didn't have to explain it to anyone.

He was dry enough not to be questioned about it by the time he knocked on Bowers's door. Sandy himself opened it with the plain, friendly manners of a miner, showing surprise when The Major asked if he could buy a horse and saddle.

"Out in the middle of no place?" Bowers asked. "You sure didn't walk here. Where'd you come from? How'd you get here?"

Dorne had no wish or reason to tell the truth. Bowers wouldn't believe it, and he didn't want him to. He gave a rueful shrug. "I was drifting through to Carson, found a shady spot for a rest and some grub. Some louse stole my horse and my gear while I was asleep. Not that I had much. I been down on my luck."

"The hell . . . whereabouts?"

"About five miles down the road."

"Hot walk." Bowers stood out of the doorway. "Hot walking in this sun. Come in. Set a spell and have a drink."

"Sounds welcome. Thanks."

Dorne walked in, reached for the knob to close the door behind him, then snatched his hand away. The thing was blistering. It was solid gold. Sandy laughed. It was a joke on strangers that he enjoyed. He took Dorne through a rich hall into a cool, high-ceilinged parlor expensively furnished. The Major was glad to relax in an indicated chair, to ease his still tight throat with well water and the finest Kentucky whisky money could buy.

Sandy had little to say while he fetched the water and then whisky for them both. But as Dorne sipped the whisky and looked at the older man in appreciation, Sandy observed quietly: "That buckaroo take your hat, too? I would have had mine over my face while I was snoozin'. You must be a sound sleeper."

Dorne feigned embarrassment. "Truth is, the hat was the best thing I owned. I sold it to buy the grub. I figured to get a job in Carson."

"But you asked me if you could buy a horse and saddle. I ain't heard how you were intendin' to pay for it." He gestured around the elegant room. "I worked for all this."

Dorne was ready. He didn't take Bowers for a fool. "I know, I've heard of you. I mean to pay for it soon as I can get enough work. I was hoping you might need some work done around here . . . maybe enough to pay for it."

An hour later, Dorne mounted the handsome saddle on the Thoroughbred that Sandy had insisted on giving him and took the road to the cave.

Chapter Fifteen

When Mark Dorne reached the deep cave in the mountain-side, he found Shawn Grogan being cared for by Ole. Grogan's near drowning had resulted in what appeared to be pneumonia. The Swede had him bundled in blankets under a buffalo robe and sat beside him on the floor, spooning rabbit stew with herbs into Grogan's mouth. In his weakened state Grogan was irritable that he was being treated like a child, but Swensen was too powerful for him to do anything but grouse about it. Seeing Dorne, the sergeant tried to sit up. Ole shoved him down gently but firmly.

"You stay quiet like I tell you or, py God, I knock you out." Swensen sounded as though he meant it. "Ole has experience with pneumonia. You don't do like I say, you maybe get consumption. What good you going to be to The Major? Hey, boss, I take good care of him. What happened with the steamer?"

Dorne crouched by Grogan's other side, felt the fever on the man's forehead. He was worried, but his voice didn't betray it.

"Blown to smithereens, Ole. At the bottom of Tahoe."

"The boys that ran her?"

"Not a one lost, Ole. Two may have broken legs but nothing worse."

Their expressions begged for his news. He took the time to tell in detail the events since they had parted. Swensen, in particular, was astonished at the ride down the sluice.

Shawn Grogan found a weak smile, saying: "Never tell him anything is impossible, Ole. He'll make a liar out of

136

you. Sir, you're going to rest up here a bit, aren't you?"

"Overnight at least. While I make a new get-up. Ole, give me a hand outside."

They went out to the pack horse Dorne had bought and loaded in Carson City, carried in new stores of flour, sugar, coffee, beans, side meat, jerked beef, and a case of whisky. Swensen surveyed the pile apprehensively.

"How long you figure this will last, boss?"

Dorne grinned at the man. "With you to feed, not long. You'll have to make out with game and what you can take from the land. But you can't hunt with a gun around here. You'll be heard. Can you use a bow and arrow? Make traps? Do you know what plants you can eat?"

The man look embarrassed, shook his head, and Grogan spoke from his pallet, growling that, if Swensen would let him on his feet, he would show him what the country could provide. But as he surveyed the supplies brought in, another thought struck him. "You lost everything we left you with when you blew the steamer. You had to. So, Bowers gave you a horse and saddle. What did you use to buy all this?"

"McEwan. I convinced an operator to wire him, and Mac wired back credit for a local store. Got to admit, it was a risk waiting around for the wire to come. But I wasn't recognized."

"So, how did you let Mac know it was you?"

Dorne grinned. "I just said 'a friend from the Seventh'."

"McEwan ain't a military man."

"No, but he's a newspaper man. He knows where I came from, and, furthermore, he knows about you. Anyway, it worked."

Dorne spent more than one night at the cave. He had to

make a new wig and beard disguise. He trimmed the long beard and mustache and cut his hair short, leaving some of the darker and longer strands at the hairline to comb into the wig. This time he used a swatch of the buffalo robe, taking a part from the belly hide.

Grogan had seen him do this before, but Swensen watched in wonder, especially when he soaked the combination wig hood and short beard, and put it on to wear until it dried. It took all night. In the morning, he combed the strands of his own head hair into the edges of the fur.

Swensen was amazed at his appearance. When Dorne got out a new supply of dynamite sticks to fill the narrow, vest pockets, he almost begged to be allowed to do it. He helped repack the saddlebags with paraphernalia Dorne might need for the next venture, including the vest, guns, jerked meat, and money. He asked where Dorne was going. San Francisco, Dorne told him.

"I go along," Swensen said eagerly. "I never see that big town yet."

"Later," The Major told him. "You've got a job here minding Shawn. Now here's an order. Eat from what's left in the cave, and, if Grogan is well enough to hunt before I get back, do it behind the mountain. Don't go any place where you can be seen from the road."

He showed the Swede how to reach the barricade he had blown down at the mouth of the round bowl of pasture land and told him he wanted a path cleared through it. He thought that should keep the big man from getting restless with boredom and taking risks.

He mounted Sandy Bowers's fine gift horse, rode around the mountain, and out the toll road west of Strawberry.

The busy bustle of Market Street lifted his spirits. San

Francisco was more alive than any city in the country. Peopled by the Argonauts who had crowded there in search of gold, it had risen on the shore of the great bay and was growing rich and proud with the Comstock silver.

There was no busier spot than the Parrott Building. That was headquarters for Wells Fargo, the powerful express company that monopolized Western transportation. Known locally as the Fat Cat of Montgomery Street, it controlled the stage lines, banking, and many related industries.

Mark Dorne was not at the moment interested in the building or the men inside it. His concern was with the company's green wagons as they passed it, coming from the Bank of California and heading toward the ferry that crossed the bay to Oakland. The terminus of the new cross-country railroad was over on that side of the water.

Many identical green wagons criss-crossed the city every day, hauling all manner of goods on their delivery rounds. They were too familiar a sight for anyone on the street to give them a glance on their route to the foot of Market, no one except Major Mark Dorne. He paralleled them afoot carrying a salesman's sample case. He had little doubt what they contained and what their destination was. Now every wagon cortège was guarded by a crew of Wells Fargo agents led by the redoubtable James Hume, reputed to be the smartest detective in the United States. The Major recognized him, riding beside the lead wagon.

With five million dollars in gold at stake he would leave nothing to chance. He scanned the crowds hurrying both ways on the sidewalks. Perhaps a hundred men in unobtrusive dress, spaced along the block on both sides, kept pace, agents watching everyone on the street.

The Major did not expect to be identified here in his

139

new wig. The greater gamble would be on the ferry. When he boarded, he kept as far from the wagons as possible, at the stern, with his back to the deck, looking at the receding city. At the Oakland side the blunt-nosed boat butted softly into the dock. The wagons were off-loaded and crossed the mall before the passengers were permitted to debark. Mark Dorne was among the last to leave the ferry.

He saw the wagons ahead making for the train and did not follow farther. Instead, he walked leisurely to a hotel, stood at the bar, and had an unhurried drink, one foot propped on the sample case against the brass rail. Then he bought the latest edition of *The San Francisco Chronicle*. The Overland would not leave for another hour, and he did not want to attract attention to himself by being early. He waited for the warning whistle, crossed the platform, and swung aboard the smoking car.

The train was nearly full. Many of the passengers would be express agents strategically spotted through the cars. He found a seat beside a gray-haired man, stowed the case under his feet, and lit a cigar.

The man looked him over, and said in a tight voice: "Did you see what they put in the express car?"

The Major shook his head, shrugging.

"Treasure boxes. I ought to know. I used to work for the company in Virginia City."

The Major unfolded the *Chronicle* to the editorials and read. It had been hot on the streets and was stifling in the car. There were no screens at the open windows, and, as the train jerked, slowly gathering momentum, smoke and cinders poured in from the bell stack of the locomotive.

The man beside him was garrulous. "I put two and two together. Read about that shipment in the paper. Bank of California is sending five million dollars gold coin to Virginia City. Think of it, five million on this train. That's all it can be."

The Major twisted to turn his back, to shut the man up. The passengers across the aisle were listening intently. The Major thought it possible the man was an agent, but if the man had recognized him and was baiting him, the invitation to talk might be more than just sociability. He grunted an impolite, muttered response, and turned his back. The man subsided into silence.

It was full dark when they puffed into Sacramento. The gray-haired man left the train there. Either he was not an agent or he had covered his part of the run. It was immaterial to Dorne. With the rest of the travelers The Major crossed to the railroad hotel for an evening meal, bought a pint of whisky, returned to the car, and switched to the vacated window seat.

The run across the flat land took another hour. At the junction they stopped while a pusher locomotive was added to the rear of the train. Then began the long, laborious climb up the big hill. The Major sipped at the whisky until anyone could believe he was drunk, pulled his hat brim over his eyes to block off the rays from the one lamp left burning, and went to sleep. He would wake on the instant of a change of speed.

He could not say how long he slept, relaxed, giving with the sway of the car, lulled by the *clacking* of iron wheels over rail joints. Then he was wide awake. The train was stopped. Everyone else in sight slept on. There were no lights beyond the window. Either they were paused at some small town where the population was in bed, or they were stopped in open country. Dorne stood up, and turned out the hanging lamp.

Leaning out the window, he looked back along the train. It was lighted faintly by the headlamp on the pusher. Noise at the head took his attention that way. The forward locomotive and the express car directly behind it were uncoupled, being shunted onto a spur track. The car was left there. The engine pulled ahead to return to the main line, then disappeared into a spur on the opposite side. It came into view again pulling a different express car, backed it against the train with only a gentle jolt. Then they were crawling up the grade again.

The Major's lips quirked. His suspicion of the publicity was confirmed. The ring was laying a trap. The new car would be filled with armed guards to meet him with a barrage if he tried to open it. Or would they have the imagination to plant treasure boxes in it with explosives? He would probably never know.

Dorne heaved his sample case through the window, ran lightly to the door, stepped down to the bottom tread, dropped off, and rolled into the dark brush that edged the right of way. He lay quietly while the train labored past. The pusher's headlamp swept over him. The train groaned up the grade eastward. In five minutes the siding was dark except for dim moon glow through a bank of fleecy clouds.

He smiled at the hulking express car, lonely and apparently deserted, got up, and walked to the sliding door. It was padlocked as he had expected. He went for his sample case, brought it to the car, and took from it a tool to pick the lock. It did not take long. Easing the hasp apart, Dorne crouched below the floor level and pulled the door sidewise.

A gun exploded over his head. He dodged under the car and crept along it several feet before easing his head out to see the doorway. Dorne did not want to dynamite the car, blast the chests open, and scatter the treasure. How many guards had been left to watch five million in gold coin? He drew his gun and waited for a head to appear through the black hole of the door.

It was half an hour before anyone or anything appeared in the doorway. Clouds had smudged the moon, but Dorne could make out the outline of a hat. The angle betrayed that it was on the end of something, possibly a gun barrel. Dorne held his fire. After a bit, the hat was withdrawn. He held his breath, hoping those inside would feel pressed to look farther, learn if the shot had found its mark. If, instead, they closed and barred the door, he would be left with the choice of blowing the whole car or going quietly away without the gold.

Then there was movement. This time a head appeared, and the man leaned out far enough to look down for something—perhaps a body—beneath the door. Dorne shot the head away. The dead man plunged out to the ground.

Dorne stayed where he was, listening for reaction from others in the car. There was no sound. No further movement. The door was not closed. He lifted a rock from the roadbed and tossed it into the brush. It crackled down through dry twigs. There was no gunfire toward the spot. Beneath the car, he edged under the doorway again, lifted his head against a corner of the opening. The inside was dimly lit by the moon. There was no movement, no sound of breathing. How smug they were, how sure of themselves to leave only a single man against him.

The Major lifted the dead man, carried him into the brush, brought his gun, and covered both with leaves and branches. Then he climbed into the car.

The locks on the chests were new, intricate. Dorne's tool would not open them. He shot one away, careful to preserve the working part for later study, dropped it in a pocket, and raised the lid. A match showed him sealed sacks. He sliced one open, and bright new minted pieces winked at him. He breathed in relief. Treacherous as the men he fought were, this could have been a second trick.

He jumped off the car. The siding followed the mountain contour, sloped back toward the main line. The car was kept from rolling by a hand brake controlled by a wheel on top. If that was released, the car would slip downhill back onto the main line and roll toward Sacramento.

Chapter Sixteen

Mark Dorne needed no locomotive to move his treasure car. He walked to the switch between the spur and the main line and swung the lever that opened it. His earlier raids had been harassment only, embarrassing the ring. Sinking the steamers had been a good strike and would effectively slow down production in the mines for months to come. He was making a deep impression on the powers who had ruined his family and were ruining countless other people every day. Now what impact, he wondered, would this loss of five million dollars make on Sharon and Ralston? It would hurt, there was no doubting that.

Grim-faced, The Major returned to the lonely car, tossed his sample case with his tools and dynamite inside, climbed on top, and turned the brake control wheel. The car coasted backward slowly onto the main line. When it was clear of the spur, he braked it again, and went down to set the switch so the westbound train coming through the next day would not be wrecked.

Then he climbed again to ease the brake. The car drifted downgrade. The moon was gone behind thickening clouds, leaving the night Stygian dark. At this height, the track snaked in tight curves through narrow mountain passes and alternately followed the mountainside above gorges a thousand or more feet deep. Some were steep, timbered slopes, others dropped nearly sheer, cañons cut by ancient rivers that still ran at the bottom.

Dorne pictured the line ahead. The grade had been built at a maximum to punch the line over the crest, in some places six percent, seldom under four above Auburn. In the foothills it lessened, and lessened again in the flatter ground to Roseville Junction, some eighty miles away. The long pull up had taken most of the night. He had a distance to go to the spot he had staked out. Thirty miles an hour, he reckoned, would keep the car from jumping the rails and would boost him over what dips there were.

He judged his speed by the frequency of the *clicks* as the wheels rolled across the rail joints, four-feet eight-and-a-half inches apart, releasing and tightening the brake, slowing when the car rocked toward a dangerous tilt or took a sharp curve, letting the car run free on the short upturns.

The timing would be close. If, in the dark, he overshot the place he aimed for, there would no going up again, and he could not transport the weight of the gold, very far by hand in the hours before the westbound would come through. He watched the sides, listened, hearing echoes when they passed through hills on both sides, seeing shapeless black as they roared past a cañon.

Then a growing false dawn helped. He made out shapes. Just when he was certain he had come too far, Dorne saw ahead a lift of skyline, his landmark. He had picked it as a possibility on the trip down from the cave. He slowed, and at last stopped beside the brink of a precipice. He was on a shelf where a rock face fell sheer over a thousand feet. At the bottom a river tumbled white across stones into a pool, perhaps half an acre of water dammed by a small landslide, reflecting the lightening sky. Below the pool, the river coursed in a smooth sheet over the dam. Brush and floating débris from winter floods made a slow circle around the pool like corralled animals seeking a way out.

The Major set the brake as tightly as he could, dropped to the ground, and chocked the wheels with rocks because the grade was steep, then slid the wide door open and climbed in.

The sacks from the box he had already investigated were heavy. One at a time he piled them against the door. When the chest was empty, he got out and again lifted them, carried them to the brink, and let them fall. They made small geysers as they splashed into the pool. They might break open, but the heavy coins would sink or be held in a horde against the foot of the dam. The water there was shallow, and the débris swirling over the bright coins would prevent their winking up in the sunlight, giving away the cache. Lock after lock he shot away, making trip after trip. It took hours to move it all. When it was done, he searched the right of way to be sure none had spilled from the sack from which he had made a marker for later search. He cut a green bough from the hillside beyond the car and swept away the path his boots had dug into the gravel.

Tired, he could not rest. The afternoon westbound was on its way over the high crest, racketing down upon him. He kicked away the chocks, climbed to the brake wheel once more, and rolled on down. His smile was tight as he thought of the consternation in high places. He was known as a loner. Not the least of their confusion would be the puzzle of how one man could make two tons of gold vanish overnight.

Without that weight to add to the pull of gravity, the car was not as steady. Dorne took caution on the curves. Lower down the grade was less sharp, and there were straightaways where he spun the wheel and let the car run free. One of these passed through a small camp, a stretch where the track was nearly level. He needed momentum to cross it, climb the rise at the far side.

The car flashed down. Then at the base of the dip, a

wagon pulled across the tracks. He whipped the wheel, heard the scream of iron on iron, and knew hot sparks were flying under the wooden car. If they set it afire—his dynamite lay inside.

But he had to slow in a hurry or run down the wagon and its driver. The driver heard the scream of metal on metal, looked, then whipped the horse. It jumped ahead. The express car grazed the rear wheel but did not overturn the box. Dorne spun the brake control again, released it to the full. He had lost speed in the middle of the town. The car rolled on sluggishly into the rise, almost stopped, then barely coasted over the rim and picked up momentum on the downgrade.

The station agent and two railroaders had run from the little building as the car screamed, watched it drift past, frozen in bewilderment, then ran after it, too late to catch it.

Mark Dorne saw the agent snatch out a gun. He dropped flat before the man fired, then hoped he was a better agent than he was a marksman as the bullets drummed into the rear of the car below him. No one came after him. The downgrade was steep. He left the brake off to outdistance pursuit, if it should come, scrambling down to look for flames against the floor. If the car tipped over now, he would have to jump. But it did not, and there was no fire.

It was after five o'clock when he reached the branch track at the junction, only an hour ahead of the westbound flier. He dropped off the moving car, ran to throw the switch, and there was just enough momentum left to glide the car into the siding. He opened the switch for the coming train, went for his sample case, left a medallion in one chest, and walked on into town.

Roseville Junction was a busy place. The railroad shops

and roundhouse were there, the boarding houses for the workmen, stores to serve them, salesmen visiting the lucrative stop. No one paid any attention to the tall, coarse-haired stranger with the sample case. Dorne walked into the hotel bar, ordered a beer, took it to a table, and sat writing a letter to Arthur McEwan of the *Enterprise*. When he had mailed it, he took an early supper in the dining room that would be mobbed by travelers when the incoming train stopped.

He heard the westbound arrive at six and the clamor below as people hurried to eat in the half hour allotted them. That train would not carry his letter. The morning eastbound would pick it up. Dorne bought a ticket west, rode to Sacramento, and laid over for the night.

At daylight, he picked up the horse he had left at the livery there and turned it toward Placerville. He rode without hurry, allowing time for McEwan to run his story and the edition to reach the Strawberry station. Three days later he bought the paper and took it on to the cave.

Shawn Grogan was on his feet, mending fast. Ole Swensen announced proudly that he had cleared a wide path through to the pasture bowl, but he'd been careful not to make it easy enough that the mules could wander away. There was plenty of food and shelter for them. Dorne complimented him on his foresight.

Then he gave the *Enterprise* to Grogan to read aloud. McEwan had set the entire front page with the biggest woodblock letters in the shop.

MAJOR HITS AGAIN
FIVE MILLION GOLD SHIPMENT TAKEN

Mark Dorne had known that no one in the ring would

admit having set a trap that failed. They would hope to keep the loss secret. But he wanted it known, and his letter had resulted in just what he wanted and expected from the fearless newspaperman.

Reliable information comes to us that the Bank of California and our local barons of finance, made desperate by the man known as The Major, concocted an elaborate scheme to end his forays. The latest of these was the destruction of the steamships *Daisy* and *Poppy* which hauled timber across Lake Tahoe. The gentlemen laid a trap baited with five million dollars in gold coin. Shipment of this huge sum was publicized widely. It was reported this gold would be sent to Washoe by the new railroad as far as Reno, thence by coaches up the mountain. The gold was loaded openly, locked in an express car. What was not made public was that somewhere short of Reno that express car was left on a siding and replaced by another. This car was loaded with identical treasure chests, but these contained rock and explosives wired to blow apart anyone who tampered with the lids.

Our conspiring gentlemen waited in confidence. Picture, if you will, their chagrin when the bogus car arrived in Reno, untouched. The *Territorial Enterprise* has learned that the gentlemen, with unusual concern for the safety of the populace, arranged that these chests be moved with great care into the desert and detonated from a distance by rifle fire. The gold-laden express car? It was found later on a siding

at Roseville Junction, the door open. The treasure chests were there. Empty. With one excep-
tion. One chest contained a silver coin of a mold
becoming too familiar to certain men of Croesus
wealth. May we editorialize that this bit of metal
is a greater bomb than chests rigged to kill a
single man. The five million dollars in gold
coins? It has vanished!

Shawn Grogan finished on a burst of laughter. He and
Swensen swung on Dorne with the hungry demand,
"Where is it now?"
Mark Dorne described the pool. "It will keep there until
we're ready to take it out. Now see this other story."
On the second page McEwan wrote of a battle shaping
up between Sharon and four new Irishmen who had dared
to move onto the Comstock to challenge the ring's control
of the mountain. Flood, Fair, O'Brien, and Mackay, two of
them mine superintendents and two saloonkeepers turned
stockbrokers, had got hold of a strip of ground Sharon had
thought barren and struck a bonanza to rival anything the
ring controlled. Now they were pressuring the ring's mines,
raiding their stocks, selling them short to break the market.
Loss of the five million dollars worsened Sharon's situation.
"They're hurting now," The Major said. "Tomorrow
we'll see what the San Francisco papers say."

Wearing his brown wig, Dorne visited the Strawberry
station, bought a *Chronicle*, and found a story that took him
in haste back to the cave. Wells Fargo was hiring what
amounted to a literal army to comb the mountains for The
Major and the lost gold.
"They'll come through here in a matter of days," Dorne

warned. "And I don't want this place found. Ole, go up above, drop three trees, put them down where they cover the cave mouth and the shelf out front. Take those with the fullest tops and tangle them in each other."

Grogan protested. "Suppose they discover it anyway. Major, we'd be caught cooped up here with no way out. That don't sound too smart."

Dorne gave him a twisted smile. "It wouldn't be, if we were here. We won't be."

"But where else is safe unless we leave the country?"

"We'll be invisible. In the middle of the search, we'll hire on with Wells Fargo and go looking for ourselves."

The idea delighted the sergeant, but Ole Swensen looked worried, asking: "There'll be some questions, who we are, where we come from, and I hear that head man, Hume, is sharp as they come. I don't know as I could fool him."

"Even Hume," Dorne promised, "sees what he expects to see. We'll have good references. I'll get them from Adolf Sutro. You two drop that screen over this place, then go to Sacramento separately. I'll meet you later at the Golden West Hotel."

Mark Dorne left them, rode to Virginia City, walked boldly into the International, and climbed to the tunnel promoter's suite.

At his knock, the Prussian called: "Who is it?"

Because the man might not be alone Dorne answered: "Telegram, Mister Sutro."

When the door opened, Dorne put a finger across his lips, saying in a low tone: "It's Major Dorne. Is anyone with you?"

Sutro's eyes narrowed. "You're an impostor," he snapped, backed off, and tried to shut the door.

Dorne had a foot in the way. He smiled and lifted the

beard from his chin to let the man recognize him. Sutro's mouth dropped open. He caught The Major's arm and tugged him inside, looking along the hall, then closed the door and put his back against it.

"You're crazy to come into this town. It's an armed camp. If they catch you now. . . ."

"I mean to see they don't." Dorne's voice was flat. "And I need something from you. You have read that Wells Fargo is raising an army to run me down? I want references from you for myself and two others so there'll be no suspicion when we apply to join that army."

The tunnel man stared, unbelieving, saying hoarsely: "Join them? For God's sake why?"

"Because I can't stay in the mountains with that many people prowling through them. Somebody would stumble on us. But as a special agent for James Hume, who's going to look at me twice? Do you know him?"

"Yes . . . yes, I do, very well."

"Will you give me a letter of introduction? As Jonah Hunt, who has been a Kansas sheriff with a reputation and who, with two former deputies, wants to join the hunt for the dangerous train robber."

Adolf Sutro reached for a chair and sank into it before his legs should give way under him. His words came on an out rush of breath. "The audacity. The conception. Yet it is outrageous enough to succeed. Very well." The eyes turned suddenly merry and sly. "I have already had some part in this business. I am an expert on explosives. A very reluctant Bill Sharon had to come to me to learn how to get rid of his damned charged chests. The man they hired to prepare those chests had left town. He'd used black powder and rigged a device to blow it. Sharon wasn't sure about asking anybody else and had to come to me. It was most satisfying."

Dorne laughed in surprise. "Then it was you who tipped Art McEwan about the way they took care of the dummy chests?"

"Another pleasure. Major, what did you do with the gold?"

"It's better that you do not know that. I trust you, but you're safer without that secret. The bank crowd is fighting you now. They could wreck you if they got an inkling you had the knowledge."

The Prussian looked embarrassed. "Of course, I didn't think. I asked out of my amazement that you, alone, could make off with tons and leave no trace. Now to the letter."

He went to the desk beside the window, laid a paper on it, and picked up a quill, holding it poised before he wrote.

"Jonah Hunt, eh? Join a hunt . . . you have humor too." The quill scratched the message, Sutro quoting as he put the words down. "James Hume, Esquire: May I commend to you, Mister Jonah Hunt, a law officer with a fine record in Kansas. I have known him some years and can vouch that he is eminently capable. He and two former deputies are anxious to lend their talents to you in the search you are organizing."

He signed the letter, sanded the page to dry the ink, and handed it across the desk. "Take care this shall not be your death warrant. Good hunting."

Dorne shook the offered hand, tucked the paper in his pocket, and left. He rode the length of C Street, then continued to Reno to take the train to San Francisco.

The Wells Fargo building was swarming with men coming and going, an uncommon number even for the busiest place on Montgomery, and, inside, the normal crowd lined the counters. Mark Dorne waited in patience for his turn, then asked to see James Hume. The harried clerk barked that Mr. Hume was extraordinarily busy. Dorne did not insist but asked that his letter be taken to the detective chief. The clerk sent a runner with it and went to the next customer. The boy was back in minutes, beckoning. Dorne trailed him up a flight of stairs to a door the boy held open, then closed it after him.

At a cluttered desk sat the man most dreaded by those Wells Fargo wanted tracked down. He dropped what he was working on, lifted Sutro's letter, and fastened gimlet eyes on his visitor.

"You're Hunt? Yes, I can use you. Use every man I can find who can handle a gun. Where are these deputies?" The voice was precise and icy, accustomed to command.

Dorne drawled: "In Sacramento, waiting to hear if we get the jobs."

"You certainly do. The three of you. One-twenty a month, furnish your own horse and arms. Report to Ed Lord at 'Cisco. You know where 'Cisco is?"

"I came through it on the train."

Hume said nothing more, scrawled the one word, **hired,** at the bottom of Sutro's letter, tossed it toward Dorne, and dropped his eyes to the papers before him. The interview was closed.

The Major wired Grogan from the Oakland railroad station to have the Sacramento Wells Fargo people put their horses and one rented for him aboard a freight car to tie to the overland when it came through. He would ride the same train, and they would go on to 'Cisco together. Then he killed an hour in a bar, waiting for the train.

In Sacramento he debarked and watched the horse car jockeyed by a switch engine, coupled at the end of the train. Grogan and Swensen came down the platform. Dorne moved away from the travelers gathered to board, and, when the pair came up, he said in an undertone: "Grogan, you are now Riley, Shawn Riley. Ole, you are Oscar Johnson. I was sheriff in Lawrence, Kansas for six years. You were my deputies. I'm Jonah Hunt. What's the cave look like?"

Towering above him, the Swede leaned down so he would not be overheard, his grin wide. "Like the biggest squirrel nest in the world. A chipmunk can't go through the deadfall we piled up there. You couldn't find it yourself. We rode out, then went back, and couldn't see a thing."

"Good going. Now get on the smoker and don't talk."

As soon as the train was out of town, the dark was intense. He had hoped to point out the pool where the gold lay, but in the black night he would not know when they passed it. Dorne pulled his hat down and went to sleep as an example, lulled by the rocking of the car and the rhythm of the wheels. He was getting to be a regular passenger on this route.

They jolted to a stop before daylight. 'Cisco was two dozen buildings, half of them abandoned until two days ago. When the road was being built, ten thousand coolie Chinese had crowded into the little valley at the right of the tracks. Now, only a few railroad men, the station agent, and the family that ran the company hotel lived here year around. But this morning the town was again swelled to bursting as headquarters for James Hume's searchers. Another fifty got off the train with Dorne's party.

A switch engine shunted the horse car onto a spur against the new loading ramp just built for unloading the gathering army's animals. When the door was slid back, The Major and his deputies brought out their horses, saddled them, grained them, then went back to the saloon that showed the only light in the area.

Chapter Seventeen

The room was big, of rough construction, undecorated except by bottles and glasses racked behind the splintered counter. Originally designated as a recreation center for the brawling crew celebrations at the end of days spent laying rail, it had not been so much as swept out since. Débris carried in by pack rats, layered over old sawdust, made the footing like walking on twigs in a forest. It was crowded, alive again, loud with arguments and boasts. Hard-faced men milled against the bar. Others filled two of the three poker tables at the rear.

The giant Swede shouldered in front of Mark Dorne, roughed a path through to the bar, and yelled at the man behind it. When the bartender looked toward them, Dorne raised his voice above the gabble.

"Ed Lord . . . where do we find him?"

The man jerked his head down the bar. From a cluster farther along, a fair-haired man with startling blue eyes raised his head and shoved forward.

"I'm Lord, who are you?"

"Name's Hunt. Hume sent us up, said to take orders from you."

The blue eyes raked over them. "Yeah, I had a wire from him."

He was cut off as a drunk grabbed his arm, spun him, hiccoughed in his face, and grinned. "Hey, Lord, tell me ag'in how much he's worth to catch."

Ole Swensen reached for the man's shoulder, picked him up, and threw him away. He landed, flailing, against a tight

157

group, and a fight started there.

"Hell," said Lord, "can't hear yourself think." He reached across as the bartender hurried by, snagged his shirt. "A bottle. Glasses . . . four."

The bartender nodded, skidded the order onto the counter, and rushed on. Lord pronged the glasses in one hand, the bottle in the other, looked up at Swensen. "That empty table, it's mine, get us there."

Swensen bestowed a pleased look on Lord and with a breast stroke of his big arms swam an aisle through the crush of bodies. Curses followed him, but as faces came around on him, objections stopped.

Lord sat down, pouring the glasses full as the others joined him, saying: "Now which of you is who?"

When Dorne had identified them under the new names, Lord nodded. "Any of you know the country?"

The Major shrugged. "I've been through a few times on the train."

Lord sighed. Apparently few of the recruits were familiar with the terrain. "Roughest piece of real estate you'll want to ride. I don't know how he did it. Two tons to move." He reached under the table, brought up a map, and unrolled it between them. "One thing is damned sure. He didn't push that freight car, without an engine, uphill, and there's no sign of a pack train around the siding where it was parked. So, the gold is between there and the junction. That leaves a lot of territory . . . practically standing on end . . . to cover." He put a finger on the map. "We're here now, above the siding, and we'll work down from here on the slim chance he walked a string of mules up the track. We know he didn't come through 'Cisco because he'd have been seen.

"Hope you slept on the train. We start fanning out soon

as it's light. Look close at everything, keep back from the roadbed where that pack string must have left a trail. They sure didn't fly out of these mountains."

The noise level freshened with other new arrivals pushing in, men who had ridden the same train but had gone to stake out hotel space before coming here. From their looks, the express company might be asking for more trouble than help. If any of this type did happen on the gold cache, he doubted that a single coin would be returned to the bank.

Lord left the table to greet them, with instructions that Dorne's party return here at daylight for co-ordination of the searchers, and Swensen again made a way for them to the street. Dorne took them to the livery to spread their blankets on hay that was cleaner and less infested than the hotel rooms. He figured they had about two hours of the night left.

He smiled in the dark. James Hume's regular core of tough professional agents had for thirty years ridden shotgun on the stages, moved the treasure chests across the west, and tracked down those who had robbed them. They would be a force to reckon with. But Hume, in his haste, had not waited to call them all in from their far-flung posts but had picked up this mob of untrained trackers who could be counted on to put their own interests before Wells Fargo's. Further, Ed Lord's version of the transport of the gold could be a help. Most of the men would be looking for signs of a mule trail.

At daybreak they packed their gear and walked to the meeting. The saloon would not hold everyone. They met in the street where Ed Lord made a speech, repeating what he had told Dorne, assigning sections of the railroad line to one or another detail, spacing them between 'Cisco and the junction.

"The gold has to be somewhere and pretty close to the tracks. That bastard can't possibly have hauled two tons out of the mountains without an army of help, and somebody would have spotted that for sure. It's probably in a cave or a hidden cañon or under a cutbank with the face blown down over it. Look for a fresh rock slide. Look for a fresh trail. And, remember, there's a fifty thousand dollar reward for The Major offered by the bank. Ten thousand from Wells Fargo for finding the gold in addition to a job with the company for the rest of your life for the man who turns it up. That's all. Mount up and good hunting."

Dorne, Grogan, and Swensen were delegated to go uphill. On the trail, out of earshot, The Major laughed. "Just what the doctor ordered. What we'll look for is a way into the cañon where the pool lies. We can't get at it from the top of the cliff because of the traffic on the line. We need to find the head of the stream and see how we can follow it down. After that, we can mark time and draw our pay. Bring the gold out later."

"When do we do that?" Grogan wanted to know.

"This winter. Hume will give up when it gets really cold and the snow is deep, then we can snowshoe in and bring it out on sleds."

For four days they rode up and down gorges, followed the deepening ravines where water flowed, but none of them led to the pool. In that country of geologic upheaval the cañons ran at many angles, a crosshatch where only the sun gave them direction. On the fourth night they camped in a pretty little valley beside a sparkling stream. Dorne hobbled the horses on a carpet of lush grass at the lower end while Swensen gathered wood and built a fire. Grogan caught a pan full of trout for their supper. They sat smoking while the shadows deepened in the bottom, the sun flamed on the rim, and the sky changed from deep blue to purple. Then, wrapped in their blankets beside the dying fire, they slept.

Much later Mark Dorne came sharply awake, knowing something was wrong. It was black in the cañon. He rolled out, threw new wood on the embers, and in the spreading glow looked around. Behind him, Grogan sat up.

"What is it, sir?"

"The horses," Dorne said, "they're gone."

He ran toward where they had been hobbled, carrying a burning branch. The hobbles lay on the ground, cut by a sharp knife. Grogan came up beside him cursing, shivering in the mountain air.

"Who the hell? Some of that cut-throat crew lost their animals and grabbed ours."

"No way to tell until it's light. Back up easy so we don't disturb tracks."

They went back by the fire. Swensen was up, pulling on his boots. They made a silent breakfast, waiting for daylight.

When they could see, they went back to search the ground. In the soft mud at the bank of the stream, they found hoof prints, then Grogan grunted, pointing. Moccasin prints were there, fresh, only half filled with water.

Swensen said uneasily: "Indians? On this side of the divide? I never heard of any. What are they doing here?"

"Stealing horses." The sergeant was deeply disgusted.

"Paiutes, I'd say." The Major was thinking aloud. "They sell firewood and beg scraps around Virginia City, and I imagine they've heard talk of the gold, came over the hill to look for it. They probably walked, so the horses looked good. They must have followed us yesterday."

He was quiet, thinking. It was a long hike back to 'Cisco. Ordinarily Indians stealing horses would ride away, as fast as possible, from where they had taken them. But with the temptation of gold they might stay in the area.

They hid their saddles and bags in the brush, and took the trail. It was plain enough, left by red men who expected the whites to turn back to the railroad. The going, uphill and down, was rough, and none of them was accustomed to walking. By nightfall they were in a narrow valley with steep walls no horse could be taken up.

Tired as they were, Dorne pressed on, encouraging Grogan and Swensen. The Indians, he said, had ridden much of the night before and all day. He thought they would stop before dark today. From the depth of the tracks they must be riding double, slowed because of that and should not be too far ahead. Slogging on, there was dawn in the east before wood smoke came down the draw to them.

Dorne raised a hand to halt the men behind him. As part of the act he was playing, he wore only a single gun at his hip and carried a rifle. He wore the vest, not because he expected to use it, but he had not dared leave it where it could be found. He knew his weapons were ready, that Shawn Grogan's would be, but he was not sure of Ole Swensen. Yet he did not want to embarrass the big man. In a low tone, he said: "Gun check before we go in."

Grogan started an objection, but Dorne winked at him. Solemnly all three made the inspection. Ole found the powder in his rifle was damp from his sweating hand. They waited while he loaded afresh. Then they moved on.

The cañon bent to the right. They went cautiously around the curve and saw the flicker of a dying fire. There they were—six of them—huddled close to the embers for warmth against the cold mountain wind that blew down the slot. Dorne chuckled inwardly. The horses were picketed on a line between themselves and the fire. He liked the idea they could slip the animals away without even waking the Indians, as had been done to them. He bore no grudge against the ragged-looking natives. He held a cautioning hand up to Shawn and Ole, and moved stealthily to pull the line loose, meaning to lead the animals back around the curve. One of the horses nickered, loud, startled out of sleep.

As the Indians rose up, they saw the white men at the rim of the firelight and scattered for shelter. Ole Swensen threw his rifle to his shoulder, but Mark Dorne said: "Hold your fire."

He hoped the Paiutes were only trying to escape and there would be no need to kill them. But one, the farthest from them and half obscured by an outcrop of rock, sent a shot toward them. Swensen got a nod from The Major, fired, and the Indian went down. Now, other Indians began shooting. They were too scattered and too far apart to stop with raking gunfire.

Dorne hooked his rifle in the crook of his arm and with both hands free dug out a dynamite stick, lit a match, touched it to the fuse, held it long seconds while bullets whipped around him, then threw it in an overhand arc. It exploded in the air over the red men. The two nearest the blast were torn apart. Two were flung flat and lay still. But the one behind the outcrop fired once more and scrambled behind the rocks.

Dorne had moved in one fluid spin, bending to yank loose the picket line and slap a horse's rump. The animals clattered around the bend without being hit. He and

Swensen followed the animals out of the hail of lead. Shawn Grogan dropped to hands and knees and crept the other way into trees up the cañon side.

The Indians near the fire lay quietly, either dead or playing dead. But the gun of the hidden one searched for him, ripping the trunks around him, but the sergeant kept going. He had no equal at stalking. Dorne knew Grogan meant to flank the rocks and corral the one who was shooting. He threw another stick of dynamite to divert him and cover the sound of Grogan's movement, knowing both were out of range of the blast.

Around the curve the horses were near panic. In the moment Dorne took to be assured, Swenson had two of them under control, one of the Indians beside the fire had sprung into action, heading for the rocks on the trail of the sergeant.

Above the rocks the sergeant appeared. Beside him a brave came up to meet him, swinging a tomahawk at his head. Grogan caught the blow on his gun barrel. The blade spun away. The other climbing red man jumped on Grogan's back, a knife flashing in the firelight.

Mark Dorne was already on his feet, crouched, running, yelling to draw attention. Swensen had all he could do to hold the two horses. Dorne was too far away to help Grogan with the knife man, but the sergeant needed none. He dropped to one knee to spoil the knife thrust, caught the driving wrist in one hand, the lank hair in his other, and with that flipped the man over his head in a somersault. He pin-wheeled again, landed near Dorne's feet, then was up again, diving at Dorne. The Major shot him, but momentum brought him on, butting into Dorne, carrying him down and sprawling on top of him.

The last Indian in the rocks tried to scrabble up them

away from Grogan. The sergeant caught a foot, dragged him back, and heaved him to the bottom. He lay stunned until Swensen split his skull with his rifle butt.

Sudden empty silence fell. Into it Ole Swensen, rolling the Indian over with a boot toe, said in disgust: "Scrawny critters, ain't they?"

"Poor devils, I don't suppose they ever had enough food a day in their lives. Let's catch the horses."

The Major turned downhill at a jog, stopping to gather up the picket line.

The third panicked horse had run half a mile. They found him in a lower grassy spot and had to use the line to lasso him. Then, they tied all three. Beaten by the long walk and the fight, their food packs back at the last camp, they made a fire for warmth and stretched out beside it. Time enough to go back for the packs after some rest.

Through his sleep The Major felt the sun come, felt its heat move across his face. As it climbed overhead and started down, abruptly it was blotted out. By instinct, Dorne knew, it had not yet sunk behind the cañon rim. He opened his eyes. Ed Lord was standing over him, spread-legged, a gun in his hand aimed down at Dorne's head. The Major raised his brows but lay quietly, only his eyes moving. Four other men were there, two with guns on Grogan and Swensen who still slept, the other also covering Mark Dorne.

Ed Lord's grin was cold, his voice a deep purr of solid pleasure. "On your feet, you bastard. Move slow. Watch your hands."

The sun's position told Dorne it was nearly five o'clock. He had slept through the day. He stood up with care, sounding puzzled.

"What's eating you?"

Lord sneered, began an answer, cut it off. Ole Swensen came out of sleep and off the ground in a rush at the man above him. The agent fired. The bullet took the big Swede in the chest. It did not stop him. His arms flung around the man. The gun exploded again between them, and yet the arms tightened. The agent screamed and shot a third time, the muzzle prodding into Swensen's stomach. Still the giant held him. Another agent jumped, grabbing at Swensen's arm. He was flung away with a flicking backhand that knocked him ten feet to the ground. The arm that still held the other closed harder. Dorne heard a crunching noise as the agent screamed again and went limp. Swensen let him drop, looking down his front as if surprised at the mass of blood pouring from him. He took a heavy step toward Ed Lord, reaching with clawed hands. He took a second step, then fell toward Lord, rigid, as a great tree falls.

Lord leaped backward, white-faced, and stood staring. Dorne's breath drew in, long, deep. He glanced at Grogan, who was up on his elbows, calculating his chances against the agent whose gun was pointed at his middle. Lord walked with stork-stiff steps to the man Swensen had killed. He sounded awed. "Broke his rib cage! Jesus." He ran a tongue around his lips, and turned again to Dorne. "That's one of you finished. Now get your hands behind your back."

Lord gestured with his gun. The Major obeyed. With two guns against him and dynamite under his coat he was a bomb. These men were not those he was at war with. They were unimportant. He did not intend to blow himself apart here.

With his great discovery on his mind Ed Lord recovered quickly. "Jeff," he told the agent covering Dorne, "I can cover them both. You tie our Major's wrists . . . tight."

It was like a hard fist in Dorne's stomach. The word slipped out: "Major?"

Lord's grin spread wide. "Thought we wouldn't find out? Hume's going to be mighty happy when I wire him I found you right in the middle of our own crew."

Shawn Grogan, gaping, blurted: "How the hell . . . ?"

"Did I know, chum?" The capture made Lord expansive; he had to boast. "So simple, it's funny." His eyes gloated on Mark Dorne. "We heard there were Indians over here and came to warn you people. Found your saddles and gear and knew you were already in trouble, so we followed along to help. We'd almost caught up with you when we heard the gunfire. Then we heard the dynamite. You shouldn't have used that, Major. Jim Hume drilled into us all . . . find the man shooting that new stuff off and he'll be the one we want."

Mark Dorne found nothing to say. He was caught. His arms were being lashed efficiently at his back and so were Grogan's.

Ed Lord was still bragging. "The boys here wanted to jump you right then, but I said, no, not until I knew what was going on. I had them take our horses down below here, and I climbed up the wall where I could see. Then I trailed you down, watched you go to sleep, and circled around so you wouldn't hear me . . . to bring the boys back. Pretty sharp piece of work, wouldn't you say?"

Dorne thought he couldn't have done it better himself. But with no expression, he said: "Very, but not sharp enough to find the gold."

Ed Lord was sardonic. "I don't have to find that, Major. You're going to show me where it is."

Dorne's voice was light and dry. "I wouldn't make book on it, Lord."

The man laughed, a smug bray. "I'll do just that. When a man reaches his threshold of pain and passes it, he always talks. You're going way past yours. I've had a lot of practice getting information. Jimmy Hume taught me, and he's the top master of the art."

Chapter Eighteen

With little gentleness the sergeant and Major Mark Dorne were lifted onto the bare backs of two horses, their ankles tied under the bellies, and left to keep their balance as best they could on the downgrade ride. The agents took the third horse in tow with the body of the dead agent tied across it. They did not bury Ole Swensen. Dorne protested that, and Lord laughed at him.

"Take too big a hole to dig, and he's too big for any of us to drag anyhow. He'll make a nice dinner for several cats tonight."

Dorne's face was empty, but his eyes smoldered. He had had no grudge against Ed Lord before. Now he did. His and Grogan's horses were roped together on a lead line to Lord's saddle horn. The remaining two agents followed behind, while the body of the dead agent brought up the rear. They trailed down to where the saddles lay. Dorne's and Grogan's legs were untied. They were jarringly shoved off the animals to the ground. The horses were saddled, and they were boosted up and tied again. They rode on.

Through the four days it took to reach 'Cisco, Lord did not mention the gold again. They came in at dark, stopped at the one-cell jail, and dismounted. A drunk was asleep on one of the two bunks, but Lord booted him out, roughed his prisoners inside, and stood by the grille, holding a gun on Dorne while his agents stripped off Grogan's gun belt, then Dorne's.

The sergeant was shoved onto a bunk in the line of fire behind Dorne. The Major's hands were cut free, his coat peeled off, and then the vest. The man taking it handled it with extreme care, hypnotized. He backed through the door. The other agent followed him. Lord went out last, and the grille was locked. They had not made a noon stop, had eaten nothing since morning, but food was not mentioned. Lord left a guard to watch them.

While The Major untied Grogan's arms, the sergeant wondered aloud in a whisper: "How come they brought us all the way here without some torture to make you talk? You could have yelled your head off in the hills and nobody would hear and interfere."

The Major told him: "I think he wants instruction from San Francisco. If I should die without saying what they want, Lord wouldn't want the blame."

The sergeant sucked in air. "You mean you'd hold out that long?"

"No, but Lord doesn't know that. He won't take the chance unless Hume says to. Get some rest. You may need it later."

They lay on the bunks for half an hour before Lord came back, flanked by four men with drawn guns. They came into the cell, Lord's eyes bright with anticipation, his hands fingering a length of thin wire.

Lord purred: "I just had a telegram from Hume. It says if you confess where the gold is and promise to clear out of this country for good, I should turn you loose."

Dorne gave him a mocking smile. "With a fortune on my head you expect me to believe you? Besides Hume isn't stupid. If it got out to the ring that I was caught and Hume let me go, he would be in deep, deep trouble. Try again."

Lord's lips twisted. "That's what I hoped you'd say. Now I can sweat the truth out of one of you."

"Not Grogan." The Major's voice was sharp. "He wasn't with me. He doesn't know where the coin is."

Lord shrugged, stepped past Dorne to the bunk where the sergeant sat, slashed a gun across his temple, knocked him out, and turned back. "Anything you say, Major. Now, just between us, where is that gold?"

Mark Dorne looked into the hungry face with steady eyes and said nothing.

Ed Lord stepped back a pace. "You want it rough, you'll get it." He held the wire toward the man beside him. "He's all yours, boys. String him up. By his thumbs." His gun was level on Dorne.

The four closed in. The one with the wire snarled: "Hold your hands out here."

Dorne did not move. Lord stepped in, swung the gun at The Major's head, hard. Dorne fell down, not unconscious but paralyzed for the moment. The wire was tied around both his thumbs allowing about a foot between them. One end of a short rope was hooked to the wire, the other end fed through a pulley in the ceiling that had been used before for the same purpose. The Major was hauled up, limp, his hands stretched above his head, his feet barely grazing the floor. He spun slowly.

Intense pain roused Dorne. Involuntarily he cried out. Even standing on tiptoe, the wire cut through his skin. Blood ran down his arms. If he hung there long, the sharp wire would eat to the bone. Dorne did not intend to have permanently crippled hands.

He said through clenched teeth: "Enough. I'll show you where it is."

"Tell me." Lord spoke with a snarl. "Then I'll let you down."

Perspiration beaded heavily on The Major's forehead. "I

can't describe the place. I'll have to take you there. In daylight."

Lord waited a long moment before he spoke. Even in his agonizing pain, Dorne knew the man's sadistic appetite was not sated. Lord gave a signal. The rope was slacked off abruptly. Dorne dropped to his feet and fell, face down.

Lord sneered: "Not so tough as I heard, are you? I'll be back at daylight, and, by God, if I don't see that gold tomorrow, up you go again until those thumbs pull off."

They took the wire and rope and left him on the floor, locked the grille, and tramped out of the jail. Mark Dorne lay where he was while the stabbing pains eased a little, then sat up. He worked his bloody hands, opening and closing them, gritting at the hot tingling as circulation flowed into them. On the bunk, Shawn Grogan came to, opened his eyes, and saw The Major. He dropped to his knees, staring.

"For the love of God, sir. . . ."

He looked around the cell for water. There was none. He tore strips from his handkerchief and bound each thumb tightly to stop the bleeding, then wiped the wet face. Dorne kept silent, allowing his breathing to return to normal, then raised his voice to reach the office.

"Hey, out there!"

There was no answer.

"I don't hear anybody," Grogan said.

"Good. So they haven't left a guard. Can you see the office . . . can you see if our guns and my vest have been left there."

Grogan went to the grille, put his face against it, and managed to get a partial view from one eye. "I can see the desk and a chair. Could be your vest on the chair. I can't tell for sure."

"Then we're in good shape. We'll wait for things to quiet down, then we'll leave."

Grogan's mouth turned down. "Sure we will. Just reach through the grille twenty feet and grab your vest, if that's it there, and blow the door."

Dorne stood up, sank on a bunk, crossed his knees, and held his left foot forward, a thin smile on his lips. "We'll blow the door, yes. Pull off my boot." When the sergeant had done that, Dorne added: "Get the package on the inside of the calf."

Grogan felt inside the boot top, found a slim bulge taped there, and pulled it loose. Wrapped in oilcloth to keep them dry were a short length of dynamite and matches. Grogan whistled a low note. "My, oh, my. A surprise party."

He slipped the package under the thin grass mattress and lay down, hands behind his head, smiling.

They heard the town gradually settle for the night. With all the search crews out in the mountains, it was not as busy a place as when they had last seen it. From the cell window Dorne could see the main street. One by one the few lighted windows darkened, and at midnight the saloon closed down. The Major saw Ed Lord and a group of six come out. He saw Lord gesture to one of his men, and the man started toward the jail.

Dorne and Grogan were on their bunks, apparently asleep, when Lord's man came to the door of the cell. He rattled the grille. Dorne lay quietly. Grogan half turned in the bunk and muttered: "It ain't morning yet, is it?"

The man laughed, kicked the grille, and turned to leave. They waited until they heard him slam the outside door. Then Dorne watched again through the cell window as the man reported to Lord, and the group headed toward the hotel. They waited until the bartender had left and reached

173

the hotel. Then Grogan lifted the front legs of the bunks to pry out the nails that held the backs to the wall, and put them together on edge against the rear of the cell.

Made a little clumsy by his bandaged thumbs, Mark Dorne tied the dynamite against the lock with what was left of Grogan's handkerchief, looked to see where Grogan crouched behind the bunks, lit the fuse, and dived in beside the sergeant. He was barely there when the charge blew. It was noisier than he liked, broke the glass out of the office windows, dropped it loudly tinkling down onto the wooden walkway. It blasted the lock and tore the whole grille off the rusted hinges.

They ran through the smoke to the office. They found their guns and the vest stuffed into a small closet. The Major shrugged into his vest and coat. They slapped their gun belts on, took the rifles, and jumped for the outside door.

Already Lord and company were spilling from the hotel, running toward the jail. Even though they were at the other end of the main street, Dorne and Grogan opened fire and had the satisfaction of seeing them fan out into doorways and the gaps between the frame buildings.

He and Grogan needed horses. They could dodge through the dark town and into the timber, but Dorne did not know this area well, didn't know a place where they could hole up safely, and on foot they would be ridden down by other search parties as soon as the word of their escape spread.

The livery was on the same side of the street as the jail. The hotel was between them, and more gunmen were spilling out of that. They heard the hotel rear door slam open and feet pounding up the alley behind it. That cut off retreat to the livery there. Moonlight made bright streaks of the rails down the center of the main street and glinted from the windows of the yellow station on the far side of the tracks. Dorne pointed at the little building.

"No good trying to run the gauntlet on this side. Make for the station. It's midway between here and the barn. I can cover you while you get there, then you cover me. We can reach the barn the same way."

The sergeant ran, crouched low, side-stepping in a zigzag course to present the least target. Dorne threw lead along the street to keep the agents under cover, but those sheltered by the buildings sent a hail of shots after the running figure. Grogan reached the station, flung himself around a corner, and began firing at the dark gaps.

Dorne sprinted, doubled over, following Grogan's zigzag. Bullets slammed into the dust around him. One tore at the shoulder of his coat. If one hit his vest, he was finished, and his war was not over yet. Then he was around the corner beside Grogan, stopping to catch his breath.

"We're halfway there. Now down behind the station to the other end and we cross again. Let's go."

"No use." The sergeant's voice was tight. "Look at the barn. They're already in there."

It was true. At least four guns were winking from the barn doorway. It would be suicide to try to rush the livery. Dorne considered dynamite. But that would set the hay afire, burn all the horses inside. Horses would run into a burning barn but not out of it. They were trapped where they were. Soon, Dorne expected, the agents would send a party across the street beyond gun range, to come up behind them, bracketing them in a crossfire. Inside the station they could hold off attack a little while but not forever. They would run out of ammunition.

"Sorry about this, Sergeant," Dorne said in a sinking voice.

"Well," Shawn Grogan sighed. "It was fun while it lasted. Good to have known you, sir. Hey! Listen. . . ."

From the grade above them a train whistled, coming down.

"Freight." Dorne's hope sprang up again. "No passenger run scheduled at night. They highball through these towns, but we can stop it long enough to board it. Cover me again."

The sergeant laid down a withering fire across the street. The Major ran in front of the building and through the door, then called: "Your turn!"

A moment later Grogan joined him and crouched below the rear window because firing was now coming from that direction, too. Mark Dorne found a red lantern hanging on a peg, lit it, set it beside the door, then sent spaced shots toward the winking guns across from him.

"When she slows down enough," he called across the room, "climb in between two box cars on the coupling! The moon shouldn't show you there. We can ride down to some place we can find horses."

The sergeant laughed. "We can do better than that, sir. Take the cab, ride it out of town a ways, and kick off the crew, then run her down to Sacramento ourselves."

"How? I never ran a locomotive."

"I know how." Grogan was now enjoying himself. "Before I joined the Army, I fired on the B and O. A fireman has to be able to spell the engineer, and I haven't forgotten how. I'll swing in and throw down on them. That will crowd the cab, so you come up on the tender until we drop the crew off."

The train was thundering down the grade, the headlamp

rushing at them. His timing would have to be close, to get the red lantern out on the track early enough that the train could brake, yet not so early that the red glass would be broken by a bullet. He waited until the last moment, relying on Grogan's knowledge of how much track was needed to stop.

When Grogan yelled—"Now!"—Dorne ran with the lantern, swinging it in circles, set it in the middle of the tracks, and ducked back to the station shelter. The brakes shrieked. Streamers of sparks trailed behind the drive wheels. A rattle of jamming couplings ran back through the cars. The train slowed but still overran the lantern at fifteen miles an hour.

The sergeant and The Major jumped for it, firing across the street to keep the agents bottled up. Grogan ran as the cowcatcher passed, was at the step as it went by, caught the handhold, and was yanked up.

Handicapped by his painful thumbs, Mark Dorne missed catching the tender. The first boxcar rumbled past him. He barely got a hold on the second one and was jerked off his feet. Pain lanced up his arms, loosened his hold. Then his foot found a rung, and he hung like a monkey against the car side, a clear target. But no shot found him. The train picked up speed with another clatter of couplings, and the agents, firing at him, did not lead their target enough.

They were through the little town and out on the dark mountain. Dorne climbed, crawled to the top of the car, and ran forward. He jumped the space between the cars, ran on, and jumped again to the woodpile on the tender. He could see Grogan's back as he stood covering the two men in the cab. Dorne stayed where he was.

Five miles down the track the locomotive slowed again to a crawl. Grogan leveled the gun on the engineer's head, and Dorne saw him give an order. The man crouched and jumped. The fireman followed him. Grogan holstered his gun and took the controls as Dorne climbed into the cab.

"Stop the train," Dorne said against the rush of sound. "I want to cut the telegraph line before Lord thinks to wire ahead."

It did not take long to climb the pole, break the line. Then they were under way again. They sped through Placerville and on toward Sacramento.

Chapter Nineteen

Dorne and Grogan left the freight in the dark Sacramento yards, slipping through the web of tracks. They took a hack to the Golden West Hotel. As he registered, The Major was preoccupied with the project ahead, the recovery of the gold coins. But, as he started to sign, he dropped the quill, clumsy because of his injured thumbs. He moved to pick it up and was staring at the headline on the stack of *San Francisco Chronicle*s at his elbow.

Financial Crisis Reaches San Francisco

He finished his signature, bought a paper, and took it with them up to the room. The story was an in-depth report of troubles originating on Sun Mountain. The ring's empire there was crumbling under pressure from the four Irish upstarts combined with the loss of five million dollars. A run had devastated the Virginia City branch of the Bank of California. Bill Sharon had closed the doors. Later, a rumor had flashed through the Bay city that banks as far off as the Eastern American coast and England were refusing to honor checks drawn on Ralston's institution.

This day a greater run had gutted the parent San Francisco bank. Withdrawals on the mountain and the ocean side were feared to have bankrupted the mighty house. The Major knew he had done much to bring it to its knees. Mark Dorne smiled as he read. People he did not know, who did not know him or his cause, were becoming his allies.

There was a statement from Ralston pleading for patience, insisting that the Bank of California was solvent. He swore that the drain of funds needed to finance the shipping of wheat from northern California ranches and the unexpected theft by the "notorious" Major had created a tight cash position only for the moment. If the depositors and creditors would keep faith, the difficulty would be solved in a few days.

"I wonder," The Major mused aloud to Grogan. "Tomorrow we'll go down and see how many people believe him. Ralston is resourceful. He's pulled himself out of jams before, but it could be that this time he won't."

Dorne and Grogan visited a barbershop early the next morning. Then they took a ferry across the Bay. The scene before them, when they walked up Market from the ferry, was frightening. Far from giving Ralston the time he'd asked for, the depositors were in panic. Yelling, cursing crowds filled the wide street from curb to curb. The bank's heavy doors were closed and locked, the shades drawn. Many had beaten on it in vain, and most were turning away now, convinced their money was gone and would never be returned. Mark Dorne stopped a man, stoop-shouldered and pale, and asked where the situation stood now.

The man's eyes were frightened. "They stopped payment this morning. I heard that Ralston appealed for help from other banks but was turned down. The stock exchange suspended trade on shares of mines the bank controls. You can see the panic, and God knows where it will end. Bill Ralston did more than anybody else to build this city, and now he's wrecked it. He got too damned big and arrogant!"

Inside the bank, the financier no longer sounded arrogant. Slumped in his office he told General Dodge, his director of the bank: "We're finished, George. Done for. I'll do what I can for the city. I've sent my wife and the children to Colonel Fry's house and closed mine. I've made everything I own over to Sharon in trust. He's to liquidate it all, personal assets included, to help pay stockholders and depositors, but there's not near enough. I don't know . . . I don't know." He stood up heavily and moved toward the Sansome Street door.

Dodge stopped him as the banker's hand closed on the knob. "Don't go out there, Billy. They'll tear you apart."

Ralston shrugged and said dully: "Maybe. What's the difference?"

He squared himself, unlocked the door, and walked out. The crowd was thinner on that side. They saw him, and an angry muttering rose, but they had no leader, and the big, elegant figure was still imposing. He walked at them, and they gave way, let him pass. No one touched him.

Major Mark Dorne saw him from the corner. Ralston went by him, looking neither right nor left. Tall and stone-faced, he did not look beaten. Dorne felt impelled to follow him. He hoped to see those wide shoulders sag once the man was out of the public eye. He touched Grogan's arm, and they moved forward wordlessly, a block behind the banker.

Ralston strode unhurriedly down Sansome to Clay, from there to Stockton, and on to North Beach. At the foot of Larkin, he turned deliberately into the Neptune Bath House, still unbowed.

Grogan whistled softly. "He loses a fortune, bankrupts a city, and calmly goes for a swim. He's made of ice."

"Yes," Dorne told him, "but ice melts when there's enough heat. I may have to pour on more."

They lingered on the street. Ralston reappeared wearing a swim suit, walked out on the pier, and dived into the Bay.

A powerful swimmer he headed out from shore with strong, even strokes. Five hundred feet out the strokes stopped. Ralston lay quietly in the swells, on his face.

A man on a ship anchored not far off saw him, recognized trouble, and rowed a skiff to the still figure. He hauled the inert body into the boat and rowed for the beach. People from the bathhouse ran to the beach, laid Ralston on the sand. A crowd gathered.

Someone had called for a doctor.

One came, bent over the banker, then sent for the death cart.

William Ralston, central figure of Ralston's Ring, was dead.

Chapter Twenty

The Major's war was finished. The ring was broken. But it had been costly to many people, yet not so costly as the ring's long reign of violence and the stock market riggings that had robbed the population.

Mark Dorne had one final act to complete. To recover the gold and to make it available where it would do good, instead of evil.

The work took two months in preparation and execution. He and Grogan built eighteen strong boxes, hauled them up to Gold Run, and rented a room behind the general store in which to hide them.

Winter had closed down. The search for The Major had been called off when the white blanket fell. Few people remained in the camp, and those showed no curiosity about the two prospectors who holed up to wait for spring. Deep snow choked the cañons, drove the people from the mountains, into warm cabins.

Dorne studied maps made by the railroad surveyors who had studied the terrain looking for a pass to bring the railroad through. On their maps he found a stream that paralleled the tracks in the area of his small pool and was a feeder fork into the Bear River. It was shallow and would be frozen solid.

On a dark night when Gold Run was bedded down, Dorne and Grogan loaded their boxes on a large but light toboggan and, using snowshoes, hauled it up the winding watercourse. It took a week to break a trail as far as the pool. On top of the precipice, a long snow shed had been built over the rail tracks to keep them open, safe from avalanches thundering down from the mountain above. The outside wall of the shed prevented anyone on the train from seeing the pool.

It took a second week to shovel the ten feet of snow off the ice, clear the upstream side of the dam, a third to chop out blocks of ice and expose the bottom sand, four feet down.

Embedded in the underside of the ice were many of the bright coins. Those they melted out and packed in the crates. To reach what the ice did not hold, they built fires, softening the frozen sand, then sifting it through a screen.

Within a month the boxes were filled, the tops nailed down. With block and tackle chained to a tree, they dragged all eighteen across the dam to the downstream side. By trial, Dorne found they could haul a half a ton at a time on the toboggan. The fall of the stream was a ten percent decline, in some places sharper, and there they had to dolly ropes around the trees to keep the sled from crashing down.

With the first ton lashed on the toboggan, they covered the rest with snow and followed their trail back to town. More snow fell every night, covering their tracks but making the hauling harder.

When they were loaded and almost ready for the last trip, huddled together under a tarp, beside a fire, drinking coffee, Grogan said: "I sure been missing that big Swede on this job!"

Dorne nodded. "I've been thinking about him, too."

They sat quietly, each with his own thoughts. Then suddenly Dorne rose, got his knife, and went to a big ponderosa. He began to carve big, deep letters.

OLE SWENSEN
R.I.P.
HE CONTRIBUTED

They made four trips before all the boxes were safely stored in the room, each brought in on a night when heavy snow kept any possibly curious people inside. When the last one was stacked with the others, Shawn Grogan sank on his bunk, shaking his head tiredly.

"I never thought to see the day when I never wanted to hear the word 'gold' again. But this is it."

"I agree," Dorne said. "It's been a job, but it's almost over. Tomorrow we'll see the last of it."

The Major was stenciling the boxes with the words:
WALKER TOOL COMPANY.

In the morning he went around to the storekeeper and rented the man's wagon and horses to haul the boxes to the freight station. He paid the agent, and then wrote the destination on each box.

THE SUTRO TUNNEL COMPANY
SUTRO, NEVADA

He and Grogan waited to watch the loading onto the train, to see the gold start the long haul across the mountains. There was no way he could restore the five million to the depositors of the closed banks, and, even if it were possible, it would be a drop in the bucket of their losses.

Giving the money to Adolf Sutro would make certain it would benefit everyone. Dorne sighed as the train pulled out of sight, his smile breaking wider than it had since his father's death. He pictured Sutro's opening the first box. The ex-cigar-maker would know at once who had sent it and where the gold had originally come from.

To The Major it was a touch of fine irony that the bank ring, that had been battling the tunnel company since its inception, should wind up by being the largest contributor to Sutro's dream.

Dorne and Grogan left the station. They had no idea what they would do next, but something would turn up. It always did.

WHEELS ROLL WEST

Wayne D. Overholser

Wayne D. Overholser, winner of three Spur Awards from the Western Writers of America, weaves his usual spell of excitement and emotion in these two short novels, appearing in paperback for the first time. The title novel tells the story of a wagon train making the perilous journey from Ohio to Colorado. Before they arrive at trail's end, a Pueblo gambler and his gang arrive, declaring that if the settlers want to continue they will have to pay—with everything they own. And in "Swampland Empire," Riley Rand arrives in Blue Lake Valley and announces he owns the entire area. But some of the local residents don't take too kindly to the news. . . .

WAYNE D. OVERHOLSER
THE OUTLAWS

Del Delaney has been riding for the same outfit for ten years. Everything seems fine...until the day he is inexplicably charged with rape by the deputy sheriff. Del knows he is innocent, but the deputy's father is the local judge, so he does a desperate thing—he escapes and leaves the state. He drifts until he runs out of money and meets up with two other wanted men in Colorado. Since he is wanted himself, he figures he can do worse than throw in with them. But these men are wanted for a reason and before he knows it, Del is getting in over his head—and helping to organize a bank robbery.

___4897-3 $3.99 US/$4.99 CAN

G. G. BOYER
WINCHESTER
AFFIDAVIT

The New Mexico Territory is bleeding in the throes of the Amarillo War, named for the vast estate known as the Amarillo Grant. The estate manager's *segundo* leads a group of night riders known as the Whitecaps, who use violence and mayhem to brutally clear the grant of "squatters," homesteaders and ranchers just trying to make lives for themselves. Cleve Bandelier, former cavalry officer and widowed father of two, leads the group of ranchers that the Whitecaps are forcing off the land. But Cleve will need all the strength and courage he can muster if he hopes to stand up for long against the corruption, brute force . . . and murder.

- -

Dorchester Publishing Co., Inc.
P.O. Box 6640   ___**5066-8**
Wayne, PA 19087-8640   **$5.50 US/$7.50 CAN**

Please add $2.50 for shipping and handling for the first book and $.75 for each book thereafter. NY and PA residents, please add appropriate sales tax. No cash, stamps, or C.O.D.s. All orders shipped within 6 weeks via postal service book rate.
Canadian orders require $2.00 extra postage and must be paid in U.S. dollars through a U.S. banking facility.

Name _____

Address_____

City_____ State_____ Zip _____

I have enclosed $ _____ in payment for the checked book(s).
Payment **must** accompany all orders. ❑ Please send a free catalog.

CHECK OUT OUR WEBSITE! www.dorchesterpub.com

MORGETTE IN THE YUKON
G. G. BOYER

Dolf Morgette is determined to head west, as far west as a man can go—to the wilds of Alaska to join the great gold rush. He's charged with the responsibility of protecting Jack Quillen, the only man alive who can locate the vast goldfields of Lost Sky Pilot Fork. For Morgette, the assignment also holds the possibility of a new life for him and his pregnant wife, and perhaps a chance to settle a score with Rudy Dwan, a gunslinging fugitive working for the competition. But a new life doesn't come without risk. Morgette's journey has barely begun before he's ambushed. Soon he's beset at every turn by gunfighters, thieves and saboteurs. If he's not careful, Morgette may not have to worry about a new life—he may not survive his old one.

___4886-8 $3.99 US/$4.99 CAN